THE Orc FROM THE OFFICE

The characters and events portrayed in this book are fictitious. Any similarity to real persons, living or dead, is coincidental and not intended by the author.

ISBN: 9798352500651

Cover design and stepback art by: Kate Prior

1

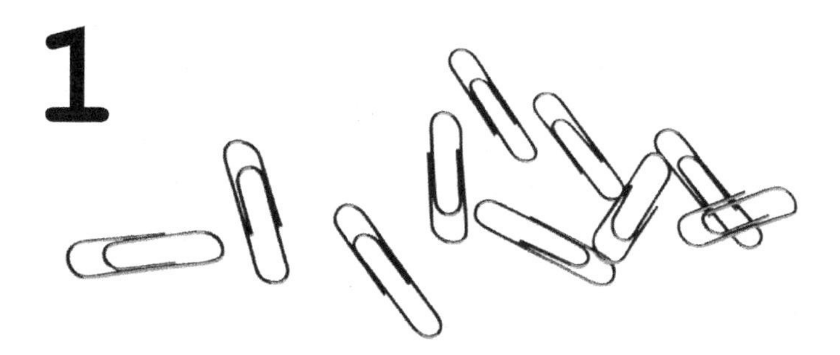

What irresponsible, fucking— ugh! Who the hell shuts a drawer this tight?!

I let out a small noise of frustration, rattling the entire metal filing cabinet as I wrestle with the one drawer that I need to stick this report in. That noise is the only hint that I'm losing my cool, and to a piece of furniture, no less.

You would think that working at a company chaired by a board of undead and a spearheaded by a fearsome necromancer, this kind of petty thing would be expected. On the contrary. I expect my coworkers at Evil Inc. to have some standards for how they file things away.

I step back, dusting off my shirt even though it's barely out of place. I take in a deep breath that's supposed to be calming.

Mediating tough conflicts is usually my strong suit. But it's not exactly my arena to negotiate with badly maintained shelving.

My day hasn't been great, admittedly, but this is pissing me off. There's no reason anyone should be jamming the drawers closed this tight. This is ridiculous. I'm about to get the label maker and stick 'Janice's drawer, DO NOT FUCK WITH' on this, just so people will stop slamming it closed and making this more difficult than it has to be.

I take in another not-nearly-calming-enough breath that makes my nostrils flare.

No, I'm not going to do any of that.

I'm going to go back to my desk and write up an email reminding people about policies regarding damage to company property, and send it out to everyone on this floor and anyone I suspect may have used this cabinet. Then I'm going to send out a company-wide reminder that performance reviews are just around the corner, so that the emails show up next to each other, and it makes someone sweat.

I'm going to cast a shadow of unease over anyone who even dares think about using my drawer.

That course of action, however petty, does un-ruffle my metaphorical feathers.

I give up on trying to pull it open, but I slap the filing cabinet for good measure, one final release of aggression.

The IT department has asked me to stop slapping my computer when it gives me trouble, but for inanimate objects, I've always found percussive maintenance to be the most persuasive. I can't exactly Bcc furniture into submission.

I do glance around real quick to make sure no one saw that completely unprofessional little outburst, though. The door is open, but I–

"Do you need, uh, help there?"

I turn around completely at the voice, straightening my appearance, all the little things that I'm constantly rearranging back into place – hair, shirt, glasses. I don't usually let anyone see me as less than composed. It's important to be a little detached when you work in HR. If you let the little things get to you, or take other people's problems personally, you're going to have a bad day every day.

Luckily for me, the voice doesn't belong to anyone I recognize.

Neither does the nearly ten foot tall shadow that overtakes the doorway.

The thick black frames on his face compete for attention with the ivory tusks protruding a few inches from his lower jaw. He takes up just about the entire doorway, his shoulders wider than the frame. He's stooping through it to avoid knocking his head on the top, and a curtain of dark hair falls forward.

He kind of hunches in on himself as he steps fully inside, trying not to bump into anything. That's a task in itself just based on how he makes the storage room feel much smaller than it already is. With how he keeps his gaze to the floor though, I can't help but wonder if there's a self-conscious element in the action.

I can see that the right side of his head is shaved to the scalp, in typical Orc fashion, revealing a pointed and torn up ear, a number of sharp looking piercings through it.

My eyes draw down his button up shirt, the way the fabric strains at those poor little buttons whenever he breathes in. The pocket protector on the left side of his shirt is wide enough to hold four different colored pens and a calculator.

He must be from accounting or something.

"It's stuck," I say, nodding my head to the cabinet. I spare a glance at his arms, which are probably about as wide as one of my thighs, if I had to guess. I know Orcs are big-boned, but I imagine there's enough muscle there for him to pry the cabinet open.

"Probably because of that dent in it," he nods, talking more to my shoes than to me. Now that he mentions it, I spot a little dent in the bottom corner. "May I?"

I nod, and shuffle around him in the tiny room to let him at the corner filing cabinet.

He kneels before it, about eye level with the stuck drawer, and gives it a tug.

Nothing.

At first, I think it's because his fingers are a little too large to get a proper hold on the little drawer handle. The second time he tugs however, the whole filing cabinet shifts forward a couple inches out of its indents in the carpet.

"No, you gotta sort-of-angle-upwards when you pull," I say, crossing over and gripping what space is left for me on the handle.

I don't know what it is in me, I just can't stand by and watch a job be done incorrectly.

I yank sort-of-upwards, once, twice—

The drawer springs free, and my elbow flies back, colliding with his nose.

He falls back, and my hands cover my mouth, downgrading my shriek of horror to a squeak.

"Oh no, I'm so sorry—" I start to say, my face turning scarlet. The mortification spreads through my body from there, heat moving through me like ink in water.

I just elbowed his face. Did I break something? Surely Orc bones are too solid for a puny human to shatter, right?

"Don't worry, it was just an accident," he says, his massive hand cupped over his nose protectively, like I might do more damage than I already have.

"But your nose, I am so sorry," I repeat like it'll do anything.

He waves his other hand to dismiss my concern and shrugs casually like being elbowed in the face is nothing to be concerned over, and not something we need to file a whole accident report over.

He removes his hand and dark green blood is dripping down his face. Some of it is smeared on his palm, and his eyes darken behind his glasses when he looks at it. "Oh, fuck."

I gasp at the sight of what I've done, and as soon as I breathe in, all the hair on my skin stands up, a storm of red flushing my cheeks.

My heart is pounding and my head feels a little funny. Not like I'm going to faint at the sight of blood or anything like that, but more like the fog of a fever taking over. It's not just my forehead, I can feel it all the way down my stomach.

"Yeah, uh, that's what I'm saying, it's bad," I tell him. I turn away, searching the room for a tissue box, but the feeling continues to bloom. There's a package of paper towels stored here, for the office kitchen. I tear through the plastic and haphazardly rip a few off.

When I turn back around, the feeling returns in a second wave. It's so heavy I think I forget to breathe for a solid few seconds. It's definitely too hot in this room for me to be wearing this cardigan.

I look at him, tipping his head back, trying to pinch the bridge of his nose gingerly with one hand and cupping the other beneath his chin to catch the blood. A drop has already stained his shirt, the fabric straining even more intensely at the buttons than it was before.

"You're supposed to lean your head forward for a nosebleed," I mumble. The words don't come out the way I want them to, authoritative, like I've got this, like I'm keeping my cool in bad situations. "Something about gravity and… oh."

My knees feel weak as I try to move closer to hand him the paper towels. They fall out of my hand, drifting pathetically down onto his lap. I don't even have the capability to cringe at myself for dropping them, I'm so physically overwhelmed, and I have no idea why.

It's then I recognize some of the sensations sweeping through my body. The desperate, aching hollow between my legs, the pulsing arousal of my clit, the fact that I can tell exactly where my nipples are in my bra now.

My blood shouldn't be rushing anywhere but my brain in this situation.

I need to get out of this room.

I turn around and stuff my reports in the drawer, before running out the door. I don't know what's come over me, but I can barely think until I'm in the bathroom near my office, pressing my face against the cold porcelain of the sink. I turn on the tap and only barely resist sticking my entire head underneath it like a woman in a badly written 90's movie. Instead I'm at least a little more mindful of my makeup. I cup cold handfuls of water to my cheeks and forehead and avoid making my mascara run.

The air in here is cool and easy. I gulp down breaths like I'd just been drowning.

When I have a little bit of my brain back, I yank a dozen paper towels out of the dispenser and soak them under the tap. I wring them out and press them to my neck. For the first time in ten minutes, I can think like a person that has manners and is considerate of others.

I was just super rude to that Orc from accounting.

"Fuck," I groan. I really just elbowed him in the face, threw some paper towels at him and left. I definitely didn't put my papers in the right spot in that drawer either.

I need to go back and apologize for all of that. He'd tried to help me, and I'd essentially beat him up.

That makes me snort a little. I wonder if there's ever been an HR complaint filed for a human knocking an Orc on his ass before.

My laugh turns into a hiccup, and then a dizzy feeling. I don't understand it. I've never gotten sick from seeing blood before.

Maybe sick isn't the right word for it. None of that was necessarily a bad feeling, just entirely inappropriate.

Even thinking about it makes me feel feverish and my heart pound.

I do not have enough PTO to deal with this.

2

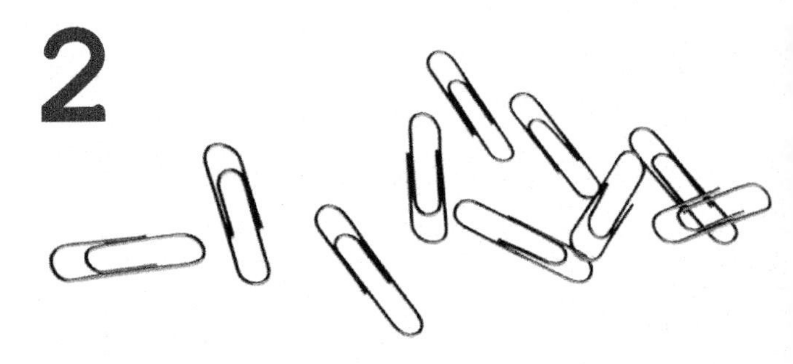

What happened this morning has been weighing on my chest ever since I got back to my desk. Normally I would have told Lily all about it during our lunch break. After all the shit I've (lovingly) given her for her mishaps at work, I'm sure would be thrilled to hear about me messing up for once. Sadly for me, Lily isn't here. She's gone along on a work trip with our boss, which, —considering their relationship, —is probably going to be more about destroying hotel rooms than it will be about work. Can't wait to explain the charges to accounting.

I'm not bitter about it or anything. That whole ordeal was just kind of stressful to watch from the sidelines. She's worked here longer than I have, but she's a bit younger and more easily influenced. I often worry about how badly the whole dating your boss thing could have gone for her, and it just reaffirms everything being in HR has taught me: office relationships are bad news.

Honestly, I'm just glad it worked out for her, because sex rituals with the CEO is out of my jurisdiction.

Breaking noses wasn't really in my jurisdiction either. I mean, maybe it is, but I haven't had to deal with something like this before.

I need to stop cowering in my office. I need to go out and apologize, but the memory of the whole thing is making me cringe. I've stood up twice in the last ten minutes just to turn around immediately and sit back down.

Maybe I can just send him a card. *'Sorry about your nose.'*

That option's not exactly dripping with sympathy, but I don't think I'm capable of writing anything even slightly outside of HR speak.

I take down my bun and redo it for the fourth time today; something to do with the anxious energy buzzing in my limbs. The complaints my scalp would make go unheard.

Maybe I can just bury myself in my job and pretend it didn't happen. Maybe it'll just fade into the background and the constant paperwork will stack over the memory of it.

Ugh, what is with me? Normally I'm the one coaching people through apologies and settling disputes between cubicle neighbors.

I grip the seat of my chair hard, until I can convince myself to push off and stand up. The third try gets me a little bit closer to the door.

I've got my hand on the doorknob, gripping it a lot harder than normally. If I let go I might just fly back to my chair, or under my desk even.

A knock startles me a step back.

"Ms. Kelsey?" a voice asks through the door, and I freeze.

It's then that I notice the enormous shadow that's fallen over the frosted glass of my door window.

"Y-yes?" I reply, my voice coming out a little strangled as I realize it's him, the Orc from before. Fuck me, he's come here to seek out an apology?

I'm not prepared for this. I need notecards and a little binder outlining the steps of what a satisfying apology looks like so I can check them off as I go, I need a powerpoint presentation to point out the steps I'll take so that I never elbow another co-worker in the face again—

No, no. It's an apology, not a meeting I'm presenting. A slideshow would be too much. But I would still like the notecards and binder.

After a few seconds of paralyzed worrying, I realize he knows my name. For some reason, that makes my heartrate pick up, maybe out of panic. Then I realize it's probably because my name is on the door. Duh.

How did he know where to find me, though?

It doesn't really matter. He deserves an apology for how I acted, no matter how weird I was feeling. I steel myself. Everyone deserves to be treated professionally within the workplace.

"I just wanted to—" he starts to say, interrupted by me yanking open the door. His eyes meet mine and he seems to forget anything he had to tell me. "I. Um. Well."

I don't really have any steps beyond that.

We stare at each in utter silence for several moments.

I don't think his nose looks broken. Bruised maybe, with the slightly darker green flushed over it, but Orc noses have such a variety of shapes and crooks and slants, and sometimes even ridges, that I'm not sure I could identify a broken nose on him. It's not bleeding anymore and it doesn't look wildly out of place.

Heat sweeps up my face and spine at seeing him. I don't think I noticed before how perfectly chiseled his jawline is, the way it's shaped for his tusks. The way the thickness of his furrowed eyebrows fucking dazzles me, it's almost absurd. I think I'm starting to get dizzy just from how lost in them I am.

We've both been quiet for far too long.

"Um. Hi," I say, reaching desperately for anything more graceful than 'I can't tell if your nose is alright or not'. "You found me."

I try to notice things about him that aren't just his looks. Example: how the blood that had run down his chin before is cleaned up.

Then I see the tape on the bridge of his glasses that wasn't there before, right above the new bandage on his nose.

I broke his glasses when I elbowed him in the face.

FUCK.

I'm going to need to replace his glasses.

For half a moment, my HR brain snaps into place. I take in a breath to offer my apologies, for the nose, for the glasses, for the pathetic paper towel pass. As soon as I do though, my jaw clenches shut and I stiffen.

That feeling is back, rolling through me with a determination to make my knees buckle. I take a few steps backwards and lean back against my desk, gripping its edge for support.

The movement startles him out of our staring contest. He shakes himself, and blinks a few times. He takes off his glasses and pretends to clean them, despite them being spotless, a cover for the fact he's talking to my shoes again.

"I just wanted to check that you were alright," he says gently, like hitting his nose wasn't that big a deal. "How's your elbow?"

I make a kind of weird, shrieky-laugh.

Normally, Lily is the only person who's heard it, because she can make me laugh and choke on my drink easily. Most people can't make me laugh. But standing in his presence makes me feel all kinds of weird, unhinged things. The sheer absurdity of this situation is getting to me.

For a moment I think about telling him, actually, no, I'm not alright. I think I'm having the weirdest fever or whatever of my life. Maybe he could call my mom for me. No, that's weird.

I clear my throat. "Peachy-keen."

He nods, his expression like he doesn't quite believe me.

That's fair. I wouldn't believe me either. My only consolation is that this will hopefully all be over shortly and I'll probably never see him again.

"That's good to hear. Uh, I'm Khent," he offers, his voice so soft and low it almost doesn't seem possible to have come from him.

"Janice. Nice to meet you," I say, and my voice cracks a little in the middle of my own name. I put a hand over my mouth and cough to clear my throat. "You're, uh, in accounting?"

He shakes his head the barest amount, eyes trained on me. "Oh, IT Department."

The all-over heat is back, along with the intense horniness. I'm just hoping he can't see how hard my nipples are right now. This bra hasn't always been the best for that.

I cross my arms over my chest self-consciously. I flash an attempt at a friendly smile. "Oh. I don't think I've ever seen anyone from IT. In the flesh."

It's true, but I don't know why I said it like that.

No. I do. It's because I'm eyeing the way the breadth of his shoulders is as wide as some couches. My gaze keeps traveling down the buttons on his shirt one by one, and I have to pinch myself to flick my eyes back up each time I hit his belt buckle.

Ogling the shape of his pants in front of him, after I've beaten him up just seems like a bad idea, but I can't stop. My sense of composure is melting under my own body temperature.

Could I have— no, actually, it's too ridiculous to even consider. Humans don't go into heat.

Khent's standing in my doorway, with no apparent intent to cross the threshold, his hand holding onto the doorjamb. I realize then his grip is splintering the wood, like he's hanging onto it for dear life.

He's starting to breathe more heavily too, sweat beading on his skin. I watch him tug on the constraints of his shirt collar. "Usually I'm down on the fourth floor, but I had to run some things upstairs earlier. Setting up some new equipment in a meeting room."

I swallow once, maybe twice. Is it … possible that whatever fever I've got, could have spread to him too?

"And that's how we bumped into each other," I say, like it's some kind of conclusion or explanation. It answers nothing, really.

Khent nods, our strange little non-apology of a conversation coming to an end.

My teeth worry into my lower lip. Just get this apology over with and then kick him out and lock the door. Then I can take care of this. Even the thought of being alone and finally able to touch myself makes my heart pound harder.

No, that's insane. I can't masturbate at work. In the HR office. Get a grip, Janice. And not on him, I try to tell myself. I cross my legs, squeezing them together for the barest amount of relief. Either my legs are really sweaty or I'm so wet it's soaked through my underwear.

For a moment I think I see his nostrils flare or something. He starts to nod, and one of his buttons pops off his shirt due to how deeply he's breathing.

It lands on the carpeted floor between us. I blink a few times.

"Oh. Um. I have some safety pins for when I lose buttons," I say, turning around and rifling through a drawer. It's something to take my mind off of the ever-growing need between my legs.

I cross my small office to him, reaching my arms up to stick the pin through the buttonhole, to close his shirt back up.

"Really, that's alright," he says, waving away my offer, but my fingers are already curling under the seam when the back of my knuckles graze his skin.

It's not a spark, but there's some kind of sensation that makes my chest jolt. Goosebumps rise up on my arms.

The touch of his skin is a powerful sensation. All my nerves seem to gather into that point of unmitigated contact between us. I don't think I've ever been so acutely aware of what it's like to touch someone.

The pin stays stuck in the fabric, whatever my intent was with it long gone. My hands fall from it, flattening out against his middle.

Before I can even think, my hands are drifting down his chest, opening up the rest of his shirt like mere curtains. His body is entirely bound in tight muscle and an unreal number of abs. My hands draw up his skin, tracing the cut of his hips. His breath catches on a note of want, and I move a hand to his arm, feeling the sheer amount of coiled strength. My fingers curl up in the fabric of his sleeve, separating me from him.

I want to pull his shirt all the way off, but the realization that I would probably need to stand on a chair to accomplish that much snaps me out of it.

I can't believe I did that. That's completely unlike me. But the need to touch and explore overwhelms every other sense I have. I feel the rise and fall of his chest against my palm, a sharp spike of temperature under my hands. There's no question, he has this fever too.

It doesn't make sense, but my head feels heavy and sluggish unreal against this. How could we both have come down with the same virus so quickly? And why is it making me horny? Fevers have never felt like this before.

As I continue to touch, to trace the shape of his torso, the heat of his skin melds with mine and makes a shiver roll through me.

I shouldn't be doing this. I would never do something like this.

I push back from him, catching myself on the edge of my desk again.

A stronger wave of arousal hits me. I've never felt it like that, so all-encompassing that I almost forget where I am. Without thinking, without care, my hand goes straight to my legs to touch myself, to find some kind of relief.

Distantly, Normal Janice is shouting something about rules and professional environments.

I don't know her anymore.

Pleasure grips my body with tension and I can't stop stroking through the fabric, even though I know in the back of my head that this incident is at least a G-2B form filled out in triplicate, and two different interpersonal training sessions. No amount of paperwork is preventative enough.

Khent finally ducks through my doorway and is just towering as he stands to his full height. Something in his manner shifts. The way he holds himself, no longer attempting to minimize the space he takes up. He's holding my stare now.

His shadow falls over me and all rational thought I have exits the building.

A low growl escapes him, the sound connecting immediately with my clit.

I've never whimpered before, but I think I just might have.

The meager stroking through my clothes is doing nothing for me. I fumble to open my pants, to make more room for my hands. When I find my clit, I can't help but let out a hiss. Everything feels more sensitive than usual. I'm really wet, it's practically a mess. I can't even begin to think about the laundry I'll need to do after. Every touch makes me need to bite my lip to keep from making noise.

His eyes darken behind his broken glasses as he stands back against the door. His pants don't do anything to hide the intimidating bulge now straining against the fabric.

My fingers don't stop working my clit, not for a second. He watches, his gaze sending a shiver down my shoulders.

Each step he takes towards me is deliberate and slow. There's plenty of time to get up and leave if I wanted to, but I don't. I'm more interested in sizing up the girth of his cock through his pants. If I wasn't busy already, I'd probably be climbing him like a tree.

His silent gaze holds mine as he stops before me, kneeling down so that we're on sort of the same level.

My heart is thudding in my chest. He reaches a hand out and grazes it against my ankle. The warmth of his hands alters something in me, maybe my sense of propriety.

His glance goes from my ankle, up my leg, back to my eyes.

I want more of his touch, in any capacity. In this moment I desperately want it. I nod.

He kneels down before my spread legs, drawing his touch from my ankle up my leg and inner thigh, easing down my dress pants. I worry my teeth into my lower lip.

After a moment's hesitation, he presses a thick finger inside me. I let out a gasp, because even though his fingers are about as thick as some of my smaller toys, it's still not enough. The pleasure that rolls through me from that one touch is overwhelming.

He removes the hand, breaking a string of my wetness as he brings it up to his mouth. His dark eyes stare down mine as he draws his tongue over his finger to taste me. I can't help but moan.

Feverishly, I nod. I want whatever he's asking to do.

His enormous hands curl around my hips and push me back on my desk, as he bends forwards to meet his mouth against my sex and I can't help but cry out. His mouth is so warm, and his hands are so hot against me, gripped around my thighs as he drags his tongue over me, from cunt to clit. Oh Evil Overlord, I am very much here for this.

His tongue doesn't feel the way human tongue does against me. I can't quite place what it does feel like. There's a ridged texture along the tip that stops my ability to think in its tracks whenever he passes over my clit.

His movements against me are greedy and ravenous, tasting everything. My hands delve into his hair and curl into fistfuls to anchor him there because I don't think I ever want him to get up. I want to live in only this moment. I can't believe I ran out of the storage room earlier and nearly missed this.

He groans and stiffens for a moment, his fingers digging bruises into my ass, before he shudders. All the while he never stops, his large, hot, ridged tongue working in and out of me between sucking my clit. I try to lift my head to peek up at him. Did he just cum? The thought barely registers before a wave of pleasure overtakes me and an orgasm shudders through me, and I'm convulsing against his tongue.

Around this point at home, I would have clicked off my vibrator and been done. But he keeps going, dragging out my climax. All I can do mid-orgasm is gasp for air and whimper. My hips buck violently into his mouth, and thank fuck his tusks are relatively blunt.

"Shhhh. Shush. Shh," is the best I can manage to say, because my brain has misplaced the word 'Stop'. I feel like I can't move now, my body has been completely rocked to the core. Every additional stroke makes me twitch and moan again.

I have just enough sense to yank up on his chin. I find my foot to prod at his shoulder. That makes him back away.

With my clit this sensitive from his licking, I feel like I might come again just from his breath ghosting over the wet mess of my cunt.

My grip loosens on Khent's hair and it slides out of my grip. He pulls back, all tall, dark and green, watching me.

Suddenly we're not the only beings in the world anymore, consumed by some weird feral haze. We're just coworkers again.

I'm sure I still look bewildered, looking back at him.

I don't have questions.

It's more of just one question, 'what?' Only with a thousand more question marks after it.

Specifically, it's a Windows 98 error noise. Just repeated over and over. I can't think of how to ask anything more specific, because I can't imagine what the answers could possibly be.

The feverish need to get railed has quieted to a dull sensation.

Even without being overcome with sensation, my brain stalls and stutters. Everything I observe or think is met with a flat 'no', but simultaneously my mind refuses to provide another explanation for what is going on.

My office looks pretty normal to me. Khent is fixing his popped button with the safety pin. He isn't breathing as heavily as he was before either, no longer taxing the tensile strength of his shirt.

I kind of look at myself, sprawled out over my desk, pants half off and my cunt a wet mess of his efforts.

Somehow I find my voice and stutter until words form. Most of them are useless.

"Um. Hi. Oh, wow. Ok. Hello. Can you, like, hand a girl a towel? I don't think I can process anything unless I get dressed again," I ramble. "You said you were from the IT Department?"

Khent slowly nods. "Yeah. Fourth floor."

"Well, this is the sixth floor," I point out, because pointing out he's on the wrong floor is easier than dealing with whatever just happened. I just have to be correct about something right now.

My eyes dip down to where his staggering boner had been before, and the lack of a cum stain on his pants is gas lighting me. He must have some pretty stellar underwear on, I'm honestly kind of annoyed by it.

Khent pauses his search for something resembling a towel in my office, glancing back to me in what can only be described as sheepish. "Yeah, about that … I need you to come to Monster Resources with me."

3

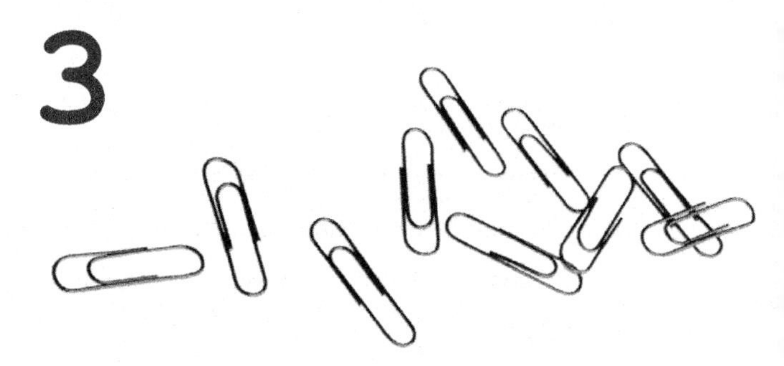

I open and close the pamphlet the Monster Resources lady handed me, glancing over it again. '*So You've Mate-Bonded with a Coworker*'.

I can't even finish a single thought. I feel my brain bluescreening on me. What kind of special hell is this?

Most of the information inside is about company policy, that mate-bonding is highly discouraged on company property. A lot of it is about trying to let MR know about any mating/bonding plans before it happens, rules for making sure a bonded pair don't work within the same department to avoid favoritism. It reads a lot like the internal dating policy the company has for HR.

The problem is, the whole outdated looking thing assumes that this was on purpose.

"I didn't bond with anyone," I say, running through this morning's events in my head again. That moment in the storage room was the first time I ever saw Khent.

Even his name makes my cheeks burst into a streak of red. I feel him shift out of the corner of my vision, and I steel myself to not turn to glance at him.

All of what just happened may be wholly inappropriate, but it was not mating.

Mating bonds are usually a bite, I think. There's blood exchange for vampires, that's done with a bite, there's the mid-sex mating bite for werewolves, there's the… well I can't think of any others but that's how it usually goes. I'm pretty sure.

Anyway, I haven't bitten or been bitten by Khent, to my knowledge. I definitely elbowed his nose, not his teeth. And for all his mouth was on me a little while ago, that was purely tongue.

Gwen, the Monster Resources lady, smiles at me, nodding sympathetically. Her platinum blonde bob sways and highlights an unnatural sharpness of her cheeks.

"Stanley's getting me the training video, I think it's a little more relevant," she says placatingly. If she's a monster, I can't tell what kind.

“Right,” I nod. I look down the conference room table, to the far end where Khent is seated, and curse myself for allowing it. He looks the picture of any office employee, all neatly prepared again, aside from the bandage on his nose.

I cleaned up after that little encounter we had, but even glancing at him makes the need between my legs thrum back alive, as if I didn’t just come like a freight train twenty minutes ago.

The room’s pretty big. I guess it’s usually reserved for large meetings. Gwen led us in a few minutes ago and directed us to sit as far apart as possible.

Gwen crosses to my end of the table, and takes the chair next to me. She lays out a notepad before her and uncaps a pen. “So, I understand you broke Khent’s nose earlier today?”

“It was an accident!” I blurt out, sitting forward. “He was helping me with a stuck drawer. I don’t understand what that has to do with this—”

I flutter the pamphlet at her as agitatedly as one can flutter a pamphlet.

Gwen looks tranquil and unfazed as she jots down a few notes. “But you gave him the nosebleed, not the drawer itself, yes?”

“Yes.” Khent's voice cuts in from the other side of the room, like he's late for something and could get through these answers quicker or easier than I could.

"And I apologize for that, I am truly sorry," I insist at the table before me. My palms are starting to sweat. I put my cheeks in my hand, my elbow on the table, my fingers partitioning my vision from him. In a lower tone I say to Gwen, "If he wants me to pay to fix his glasses, I'll figure out some way—"

"Not to worry, that's covered in the Monster Health Plan, it happens more often than you think," she says easily. She points her pen towards my outdated pamphlet.

"Drawing blood is an Orc betrothal custom. Apparently, it has roots in some kind of physiological response. Blood Fever or something it's called," she shrugs as she writes something down. "I'd have to look it up for specifics."

"Could you? Look it up?" I squeak.

"Yes, well. Here's the movie now. I'm sure it will be enlightening," Gwen smiles at me again as Stanley comes into the room, looking out of breath with sweat stains beginning to form on his thin button-down shirt. He waves a VHS tape triumphantly at me.

Fuck. It's been at least a decade since I saw one of those. I can only just imagine what crypt of company archives Stanley had to dig through to find that. Has nobody made any more recent resources on this?

The cardboard jacket on the tape is faded enough that the title isn't legible anymore. Gwen fiddles with the combo DVD and VHS player for a few moments, rewinding the tape before she turns the TV on and hits ‘Play’.

Static dances across the screen momentarily while the player whirrs mechanically.

“Well. Too bad the vending machine was out of popcorn,” Gwen jokes, and slips back out the conference room, closing the door behind me. I can't help but listen to her fading footsteps.

Khent's chair creaks as he shifts in it. I curl my fingers around the edge of the table and sink a little lower in my chair, eyes trained on the TV screen.

The beginning of the tape on Orc biology is boring and not all that helpful. I learn their blood is green due to copper-based hemocyanin, the many sets of tusks they can go through during their life, etc. I spend more than I'm willing to admit of it glancing down the table at Khent, searching for his reactions. He’s angled enough away that I can’t really see much of his face.

Then the tape gets to a part that makes me want to sink low in my chair and disappear under the table. Or even duck out the fire escape.

“Having a long history with courtship by combat, many Orc mating traditions started with bloodshed. The breaking of skin triggers a pheromone response, colloquially known as the ‘Blood Fever’, for the fever-like symptoms it starts with,” the tape's narrator drawls on like it's an interesting fact. "Those pheromones, once spread to the one to draw first blood, would calm the partner into stopping their attack, and begin a centuries-old claiming ritual."

I cover my face with my hands and sink a few inches further into my chair. It doesn't take me long to connect that by elbowing Khent in the face, I must have accidentally initiated the Orc mating bond.

I wish I could clarify with Khent's biology that I wasn't actually attacking him. It was an accident.

"On occasion, the Blood Fever phenomena has been noted to affect other species, such as werewolves or vampires, the rare brave challenger who dares to take on an Orc."

The video droned on about how combat-based courtship was somewhat frowned upon today, but that bloodletting ceremonies were still arranged between families to preserve this beautiful and unique cultural custom.

The video soon ends, and the light flicks back on. I feel like half a lifetime has passed since this morning.

Fuck. I'm mated to an Orc.

I've sat through a number of sensitivity training sessions with other company members, usually teaching them how not to micro-agress the undead, respecting the cultural boundaries of swamp creatures and accommodating the needs of cursed peoples. I've seen most of these videos enough to have them half-memorized.

None of them have made me feel like I'm back in seventh grade watching a video about the wonders of puberty through my fingers.

Still, I think I would rather have been prepared beforehand. How many other monsters could I have accidentally stapled their fingers or given a papercut? How does anyone work here, traipsing around, not knowing how they could accidentally trip into a mating bond?

Gwen slides back into the seat next to me, straightening out a stack of papers on the table. I don't even remember her coming back in. She smiles again in that way that's starting to make me despair.

"So our policy does not allow mate-bonding on company time or premises, but because this was an accident, and you work in different departments, we're not going to consider what happened as such. We do, however, have a couple policies regarding mating-bond annulments," Gwen says, as cheerfully as if she were telling me my health plan options. "Since you two brought this to us fairly quickly after the accident, it should be rather easy. Annulments are a lot harder to arrange after."

"After?"

Gwen's smile pinches her face a little. She glances around the room and makes a quick, work-inappropriate gesture. The video probably couldn't have gone into very much detail about the alluded claiming ritual if that was involved.

My eyes flick to Khent, all thirty feet across the room, and meet his for the first time this meeting. My face burns. Do we need to tell her that we've already found the time for him to eat me out? Does that not count?

"Your local pharmacy should sell some sort of over the counter anti-aphrodisiac that most Orcs use, just ask them any questions you have about human appropriate dosages. The company can reimburse you for the cost since it was an on-site accident. There's also some pamphlets on the different side effects the medications have on different species, though there isn't a lot of information about how it affects human systems."

The thought of more outdated company pamphlets giving me possibly wrong information makes me balk.

"What's the other option?"

"Option two, if you like, you can wait to see how long it takes to wear off on its own. Since you two work on different floors, it shouldn't be much of a problem. Or we can arrange for one of you to work from home," she says. "Annulment studies show Blood Fever can take a couple weeks to a month to completely leave the body for Orcs. Again, there aren't many case studies of how humans are affected."

I swallow. Trying to get on with my work day mildly horny all the time doesn't sound great, but it doesn't sound as risky as taking some over the counter magic herb that isn't EFDA approved.

I glance down the long conference room table.

Khent has been utterly silent the last few minutes. His chair hasn't creaked once since Gwen mentioned annulments.

I mean, I guess we don't really need each other's input on this. This isn't couple's therapy, I don't need to consult him on this. I didn't ask to be mated or bonded, or whatever!

Still, I guess I got him into this mess. He probably doesn't want to be in it as much as I do.

"What are your thoughts?" I ask, trying not to sound like I'm shouting across the table at him.

The light reflects off his glasses as he turns his head to look at me. "It's up to you."

Impassioned pleas, that was not.

I guess the whole bonding thing means about as much to him as it does to me.

I shrug and turn back to Gwen. "Option two sounds good."

If I've never noticed Khent much around the office building before, *surely* we can go a couple weeks without running into each other again.

4

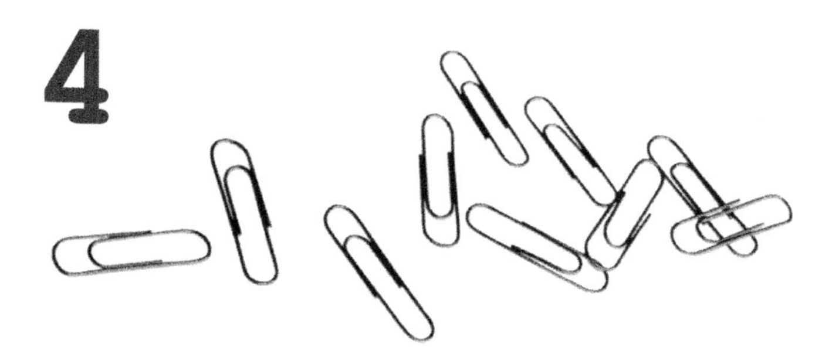

Day One of waiting for the bond to break, there's a number of follow up emails from Gwen in Monster Resources after the incident.

I kind of parse through them slowly, only half taking in what she has to say. A lot of it is legal jargon that boils down to the company not assuming any responsibility for what happened, despite it happening on the premises.

When I click back to my inbox, there's an email from Khent. It takes me a moment to realize it's him.

'Dear Ms. Kelsey,

Per our meeting with MR, I would like to reach out and formally apologize for the mess I've involved you in, and the personal nature of the entanglement. I realize it's not the most pleasant of interruptions to one's work day, and that for humans, the sudden nature of a bond can be highly uncomfortable.

While I hope you understand that I never could have seen this coming, I do hope you know how deeply I regret putting you in such a position. Thanks for coming to Monsters Resources with me to figure out a solution quickly.

Warmest regards,

Khent Rhaen

4th Floor IT Department'

I think I hate him. How dare he write a perfectly composed email about this? I nearly managed to bury the memory of his tongue against my clit under a bottle of white wine and 3/4 of a double cheese pizza and six hours of HGTV shows about people who do not deserve beachside property, and now there's an email, dredging it all back up.

And now I have to respond to this, when we could have just silently decided yesterday never happened and never had to give each other another thought.

Hell, I have a hard enough time writing regular emails. I don't know what the professional words are for 'I'm also really sorry for getting so insanely horny in front of you, won't happen again.'

Not to mention I still owe him an apology for elbowing his face.

'It's fine, really,' I write back after maybe an hour of deliberating over word choice and marinating in a puddle of self-loathing. *'And it's really my fault for getting between you and that stuck drawer.'*

When I come back from lunch, there's a short reply from him. Somehow its terseness is warmer than the formality of his first email.

'Well, you saved me from a worse fate, mate-bonding with a defective file cabinet.'

I snort, and then choke when I scroll down a bit more.

'I also wanted to apologize for the... encounter in your office when I came up to bring you to MR.'

My face burns at that line. Encounter. What a way to rephrase 'my mouth intimately buried in your cunt'.

I'm not about to get all tied up in knots over what happened in my office. I'm a grown adult. Supernatural horniness or not, I'll be responsible for my own choices to have sex at work.

It wouldn't be the first time, but I am determined that it will be the last.

'I don't think either of us were prepared for the intensity of the fever,' I type out. I chew my lip a little, before I start hitting the backspace key, erasing all of it.

Maybe it was just me who couldn't handle it. He had seemed so contained until I was essentially fingering myself in front of him.

I am ridiculously out of my depth.

And yet even thinking about that moment makes my heartbeat pick up, and travel south. I squeeze my knees together in my seat. When that provides minimal relief, I glance at my closed office door, let my hand travel down to trace myself through my pants. If I was wearing jeans, I might try to ride the stiff seam that can find my clit much better than any of my exes could.

The fever has been burning low and steady all day at work, nothing like when I was in the same room as Khent. To think it was just yesterday we were in here, his tongue dragging through my folds, giving me the most intense head I've ever had.

No, I'm not going to rub one out at work over that. I'm not going to get any more tangled up with this guy than I already have.

I send him a quick answer. *'We don't have to talk about that.'*

Then I make a point of not checking my email until the end of the day, just to avoid getting wrapped up in this whole mate-bonding business. I have other work to do, after all.

Still, when I do end up checking my inbox again, I insist to myself that I'm not mildly disappointed that he never replied after that.

-

Day Two of waiting for the bond to break, my concentration isn't much better. The memory of that MR meeting hangs over my every thought.

"Take your time to research, and let me know if you have any further questions," Gwen had leaned in and said just a little too quietly for my liking. It had made the thought of doing my own research feel illicit, instead of simply part of the process with MR. My cheeks grew hot and I had been all too well aware of Khent's presence in the conference room.

Presumably, Gwen had meant researching if there were any human sized dosages of the anti-aphrodisiacs, or the general effects of the Blood Fever. Mostly I wondered if it meant I could take extra sick days, since the whole Blood Fever incident had happened on the job. Maybe I could take a long weekend with worker's comp.

Still, none of that ended up being what I started typing into the search bar first thing when I got to my office the next day and firmly shut the door.

'Blood Fever, humans' yielded odd and mixed results, none too helpful. There didn't seem to be much record of humans mating with Orcs, accidentally or not.

‘Accidentally mate-bonded’ was not much better. Apparently there was a whole genre of Orc literature dedicated to this trope, and there were more articles on literary analysis than there were on the practicalities of the aftermath.

‘Blood fever effects’ ended up being where I stayed the longest, meandering down one article to the next.

DoctOrcs.com had a rundown of the most common symptoms, a bit of medical jargon on the systems that were affected by it, and a few at-home treatments for those who were struggling with annulments. The little warning at the bottom of the page to call medical professionals if there was blue or purplish swelling of the genital regions was a little alarming, and I hoped that would be one area where humans and Orc biology differed.

Regular masturbation seemed to be the number one suggestion for at home treatment. Then the usual methods, cold showers and exercise. Then the unusual– bloodletting was suggested more than once. I suppose there might be more than one reason the Orcs called it Blood Fever.

Some more dubious pages with less technical wording seemed to suggest there were certain essential oils that could cure Blood Fever, abscessed tusks, and cancer.

Of course, there’s only so much I can find about treating Blood Fever before I end up down a rabbit hole about mate bonds.

There's a lot of densely worded articles on the subject, half of which are all blocked behind paywalls. I don't know that I'm willing yet to subscribe to an academic journal to be able to read an article I have to look up every fourth word for. From what I get off Monstrouspedia, scientists believe there's a handful of factors: from the ages of those involved, to if the fight or flight instinct is already engaged, to hormones. Some theories talk about how they believe it has to do with immune systems being compatible.

There are other less quantifiable explanations offered up as well. There's a documentary of old, graying Orc couples talking about what they felt in that moment, how it happened to them. They caress the scars on each other's faces or arms, the strike that started it all.

"I knew it before she even touched me," one ancient Orc said of her wife, who nuzzled into her shoulder, before the documentary cuts to pictures of the two of them in their youth, "I could smell her sneaking up on me. I felt it was going to happen just a moment before it did."

That one stays with me, snags on my heartstrings and the rest of the documentary rolls by without anything else really registering.

I lean back in my chair and cross my arms over my chest, chewing the inside of my cheek. It sounds beautiful in a way that makes me feel even more like I've accidentally trampled across something sacred, and kind of disappointed that I'll never really understand what they're talking about.

Which is useless because it's not like I ever wanted to be bonded in the first place. None of this would even be on my radar if I hadn't tried to open that damn cabinet.

I keep clicking through links absentmindedly, on some balancing act between insatiable curiosity and the knowledge that whatever I do find might just make me more sad about living alone, and feeling more and more lost on every new dating app I try.

Orc women must have it much easier, not swiping left until you've developed carpal tunnel in one thumb. I wish I had that capability, to be able to just look at someone and know they're it.

At one point, I click on a video out of curiosity, thinking it would circle back to explaining what to expect when you're bonded. In my defense, that's what the title of the link, "When Blood Fever Hits", led me to believe.

But when a video loaded, I'm embarrassed to admit it took me a few seconds longer than it should to realize what it was. To be fair to me, porn is usually a lot less green. At least the porn I've been searching on purpose up until this point.

The wet smacking sounds of one Orc pounding into the other's cunt makes heat rise up in my skin from my face to my thighs. I'm caught like a deer in headlights, I'm too stunned at first to do anything but stare.

It's only when a popup ad censors half of the video, I'm able to blink and think perhaps I shouldn't be watching this on my work computer.

I should save the link for my personal computer. Yes. Brilliant idea.

I click out of the ad and start searching for a post-it note I can scribble the URL onto, but then with an absolutely primal growl, the pornstar Orc pulls out, and his massive cock takes center screen.

My cunt aches with an ever-urgent need as the money shot slows across the screen, thick white ropes of fluid gushing from his cock, leaking out of the actress. His hand continues to pump up and down aggressively, encouraging more to spill forth.

I've never been more aware how empty my cunt feels. I think I have a new kink.

I bite my lip to stifle an involuntary noise. I wonder if maybe all Orcs have equipment like that, or perhaps Orc porn stars are particularly well endowed. I'm absolutely kicking myself for not getting a better look the other day at what Khent was packing.

The rest of the shaft is covered by a thick foreskin, ridges all the way down, impossibly girthy. Only with the full eagerness of his bobbing erection, does the foreskin pull back tight, straining space between the ridges.

The head is sort of concave, supple and glistening. I can't help but note the twin slits nestled within the tip, their untempered current of release painting the Orc's thighs.

Raging erection doesn't seem adequate to describe it, not even when the Orc's hand strokes up and down his slickened cock, the last drops leaking from the tip.

Without even realizing it, I'm pressing my knees together so hard I'm going to have bruises tomorrow.

I balance on the precipice of either locking my office door and rubbing one out at my desk, or going to go find an ice pack and stick it between my thighs. It might be the only way I can concentrate on getting my work done.

My inbox dings.

An email from Khent. I don't know why that makes me salivate. In my reverie of horniness, somehow that's a good thing, even considering the last one.

I click it open without thinking, and the result is more effective than a cold shower.

'Dear Ms. Kelsey,

I regret to inform you that I have received a ping from our monitoring system that a work inappropriate website had been connected to your computer's IP address for an extended period of time. If you would kindly make an appointment with the IT Department, a report needs to be filled out, and if necessary, your device scanned for malware.

Khent Rhaen

4th Floor IT Department'

That's it. I'm going to melt my computer.

5

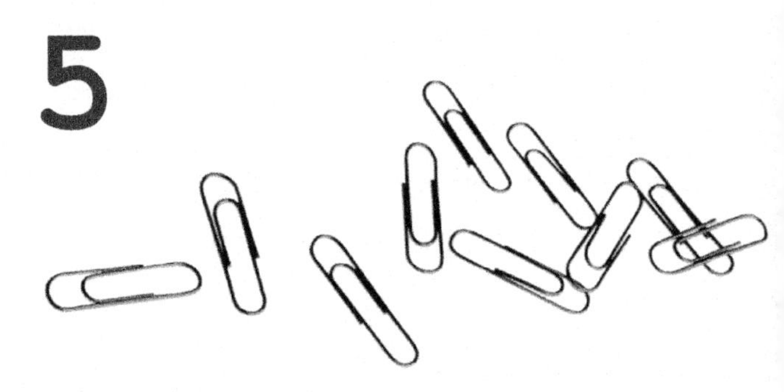

Maybe I spent the better part of a meeting staring at the conference room windows behind my boss, wondering if it would open more than a three-inch crack, or at least wide enough I can shove my computer out and watch it fall six floors, then smash to itty bits on the pavement.

"Janice?"

And then once this plan succeeds, I would go get Khent's computer, and do the same. Evidence obliterated, in theory.

"Janice."

I can imagine there's OSHA related reasons we don't have windows that open all the way, but then again I've never noticed this company's particular dedication to OSHA compliance.

"Jaaaaanice."

I blink a couple times, realizing I have been gnashing the end of my pen between my molars, and absolutely zoned out.

I drop the pen and look up at my boss. Melanie's got her arms crossed and a look of mild concern on her face.

"Thought you'd gone catatonic on us," she says, suppressing a laugh.

"Oh. No. Just, uh, thinking," I shrug, the weakest excuse I could probably come up with.

She nods to Bill. "We were just saying some of the personnel files need to be updated."

Bill continues for her, in his soft, ancient voice, like two pages of an antique book rustling together, "There's certain distinctions to be made after a tax law was altered a year ago. Some employees never updated their tax status to reflect it."

I nod along, and lean forward, trying to look engaged. "Was that the law about filing single or married after undeath?"

"Yes, I believe the part that confuses people is that if you've been reanimated by a necromancer, you are allowed to actually file as their dependent. Not everyone fills that part out correctly."

Normally I adore Bill. Honestly, this whole office would fall apart without him constantly checking that everything was in shipshape. But right now, listening to him talk while low-key squirming under the, ahem, symptoms, of Blood Fever is about as uncomfortable as it gets. Maybe I need to email Gwen about working from home for a bit, actually.

"Uh, while we're updating things, we should look into updating any outdated training material," I tack on, clearing my throat and sitting up straighter.

It is a bit of a topic change, and probably shows that I have absolutely no mind for this topic right now.

"We'll circle back," Melanie nods, though by her expression I think that means she's going to swing by my office for a little one on one time.

I leave the meeting cringing at myself, and mildly ticked that we couldn't have gotten that done in an email.

It's cooler outside the meeting room, where it felt like I was marinating in my own bubble of horny thoughts. Walking around has helped me think a little clearer. I don't need to despair over the thought of what might happen now that I've been caught searching porn at work. Besides, with our non-functional windows, my hare-brained plan won't work.

I'm not ready to chat with Melanie about my zoning out yet, so I'm resigned to pacing around the hallways and up and down random staircases to work off my feelings.

I don't think she knows about the porn search yet. She was definitely in too good of a mood for that conversation. Unless that's what she really wanted to 'circle back' to.

Unease bubbles in my stomach like a bad tuna sandwich at the thought. It wouldn't be the first time I've had to cut and run from a job. I've learned how to be prepared for the floor to fall out from under me. I always keep an up-to-date resume, I have a list of references I know will say good things about me, and I always have an eye out for job listings. Having worked in HR, I know all the tricky questions that get asked in interviews, how to dodge all the wrong answers, and the right moments to drop a couple corporate buzzwords.

I make it a few floors down before I realize I'm not alone in the stairwell, there's a voice coming up from a lower landing. I stop short when I recognize it, the sound of my footsteps echoing off the concrete walls.

I peer over the railing, catching a glimpse of Khent two floors down, with a cell phone up to his ear.

"I am not going to bring up couple's therapy. Ma, I can't. Humans don't do things like we do. Bonding isn't… important to them. It isn't a thing at all to them," Khent was saying, and immediately there's an outburst on the other side of the phone, more than one voice speaking over top of each other. Khent holds it away from his head a moment, turning the call volume down.

"Anyway. It was just an accident," he says.

One of the vents kicks on behind me, and I feel the brush of air against my skin. Only moments later, Khent stiffens. He turns and his eyes meet mine through the slice of space between the floors.

All the hairs on my body stand on end.

I have to reassure myself that I am not turned on that he can pick up my scent. I'm not. Really.

His gaze holds on me. "I should go, Ma. Tell the rest I said hi."

I look away and stare hard at the speckled concrete walls while he ends the call and pockets his phone.

When I finally glance up again, I wish I'd kept my eyes on the ground.

Even with the vent blowing cool air past me, heat creeps up my cheeks at the visible evidence of arousal starting to bulge in his pant leg. MR did say something about not being in the same room together, even if no one would consider the stairwell a room.

On one hand, it's nice to know I'm not the only one having unwarranted physical reactions. On the other hand, I don't know what it says about Khent that the scent of my hair conditioner is getting him hard.

Khent rolls his neck and grumbles a little, angling himself away so his erection is much less visible from me. I'm simultaneously disappointed and impressed with the quality of pants he owns.

“I don’t need to tell you about company policy for personal calls,” I say, a line of defense to conceal how curious my eavesdropping had made me, half to say anything at all. I cringe at how callous I sound.

Khent raises a brow at me over his shoulder, like I have any business telling him off when he knows I’ve been searching porn at work.

I press my lips together a moment and add, “But I won’t say anything if you don’t tell anyone I’m hiding from my boss either.”

For a moment, his face is unreadable. A sliver of a smile breaks through between his tusks. Then a near silent laugh gives his massive shoulders a little shake. A silent earthquake in its own right.

I realize then that I’ve been clutching the railing. Less like I’m trying to not fall over the edge, more like it's the only thing between us and if my puny human arms were stronger, I could rip my way through them. Fucking hormones. Or pheromones. I don’t know.

I sink down onto the step, trying to make myself hold the railing bars looser. I lean my temple against them and the cool touch of the metal on my skin cuts through the heat.

“So, uh, kinda soon to tell your mom about us. You haven’t even asked me to dinner yet,” I chide teasingly, and his face flushes a slightly darker green.

"I'm. Uh. Not great at lying to my mom," he admits, running a hand through his dark hair, ruining the neat combed lines he had.

"Not even over the phone?"

"Believe me, I got in more trouble trying to hide the rules I broke as a kid, than actually breaking them," Khent shakes his head, though he looks fond. He smiles a little like he's remembering something.

I'm not charmed by his mama's boy-ness, I'm just pressing my face a little too hard into the railing bars.

I force my eyes to the ground in front of me, and mumble, "Maybe you've got poker tells."

"Probably."

A silence falls over the two of us. This might be the first real conversation we've had in this whole ordeal. It's nice. It's normal.

In the last few days, I feel like I forgot how to be normal.

I fidget with a loose thread on my pants a moment, unwilling to get up and just leave. I want to keep talking to him. It's nice not to have to be the only one suffering through this, even if we have to stay several yards apart.

"So, tell me about bonding. I don't really have a reference point for it," I say, instead of telling him he's wrong about thinking humans wouldn't think it important. I'm sure it's important.

Khent shrugs. "It's just the foundation of Orc society. That's all."

I swallow. "Oh, that's all?"

I had felt a little bad about eavesdropping, but something about his tone made guilt sink down in my stomach. Not only had I stumbled into accidentally kickstarting the whole mating ritual thing, but apparently I'd stepped on some important cultural norms.

Why couldn't the pamphlet have gone into a little more detail on that? Surely the many sets of tusks an Orc goes through in life could have taken a back seat to this.

"It really isn't possible to step on another human's toes and be pronounced married from it," I say after a little while, my unease probably a little too clear in my voice. "Though to be fair, if it was a thing for us, we'd probably all wear steel-toed shoes."

He gives a laugh so small it's barely more than a breath. "To be fair, humans don't usually draw first blood from an Orc barehanded. At least, not that I've heard of."

I nod a little. The internet had turned up about that much too. "If I'd have known, I would have worn protection."

He raises an eyebrow.

"Elbow-pads."

"Ah." He nods, though it seems even with clarifying, my joke didn't land.

I scoot down a step, inching closer. I want to know more about this, what bonding means to Orcs. If it really is the same as getting married or if it's more just like a relationship. And like, even humans get married and divorced a number of times over their lives.

"So, you can just end up married to anyone that breaks your nose?"

Khent gives me a look, like I'm a silly human for not knowing something so simple, so obvious to him.

"It doesn't happen every time you get into a fight. It's something of a rare event in your life," he shrugs.

"Oh," I say, because, shit. Fuck me.

So like a more important than marriage kind of thing? Like a once in a lifetime thing? *Fuck, fuck, fuck.*

"How rare?"

I cringe at the way my voice catches on the words, but I'm far more preoccupied with hanging on every micromovement of his face, waiting for the answer.

He shrugs again, runs a hand through his hair. "Not everyone gets a chance to have it happen to them."

I wince, like I could crumble inwards on myself and out of existence.

Maybe it's not rarer than winning the lottery, but I can only imagine growing up, wondering whether or not you'd find a mate this way, and then some idiot human elbows you in the nose?

It makes me want to square up with whatever cosmic beings are out there deciding these things, to break their noses and tell them Khent didn't deserve to have his one chance at a mating bond ruined with me.

I want to tell him it'll probably happen again, with someone important to him. Someone he's probably completely head over heels for. I doubt he would believe me though, since I am clearly no expert.

"Do you know why it happens?" I venture, even though this is getting a little too fraught and way more personal than I ever intended to get with Khent. I don't know what kind of answer I'm hoping there is.

He shrugs again. "I couldn't tell you why you get hiccups either."

I nod. That's fair.

I don't really know how to apologize for being the person who robbed him of this once in a lifetime opportunity and got tangled up in his personal life in the most intimate of ways. 'Sorry' feels wholly inadequate.

I watch him for a moment, and there's something in the little ways his eyes track the movements of his hands as he unbuttons his shirt at the wrists, rolling up his sleeves.

It's not the first time I've thought he was attractive, Evil Overlord knows my hormones have taken care of that, but it is the first time I've felt on the level with him. The tousled hair and his shirt less than perfectly buttoned up, he looks like he's been having a rough time of it as well.

Maybe I don't hate him, despite my feelings about his emails. Maybe I was just mad that I was stuck in this situation and wanted someone to direct my anger at. Because as much as this sucks for me, from my recent education, it sounds like it is colossally worse for him.

I think desperately for a moment for something to get out of this personal conversation, some conversational parachute that will pull me out of this stairwell. He had mentioned in his email something about handing over my laptop to get it looked at for malware.

"Out of curiosity, where would I go to download a virus?" I ask after a moment, and then wish I'd just searched it on the internet. Still, it's the only thing I can think to talk about. "So that I know what sites to avoid. And if we're on the topic of my search history, is it like a three strike system, or is it one and done?"

Khent's forehead creases as he looks at me again. "What do you mean?"

“I mean, do you tell my boss immediately or do I have to rack up a few more incidents before Melanie has enough to fire me?”

“Fire you? No, I–” he pauses, and his brow wrinkles behind his thick glasses. “Forget about the search. I'll...if you take the phishing refresher course and pass the quiz at the end, it'll all be good.”

I wrinkle my nose. “That corny training course? Don't we already have a spam filter for that stuff?”

“It's not just for emails, it also has to do with clicking on links that look suspicious.”

I chew on the corner of my cheek for a moment. That could easily explain why I was searching porn on my work computer, I guess.

“Fine. But I want to clarify I wasn’t asking you for any favors—” I start to say. I don’t want him to think I’m trying to take advantage of this little heart-to-heart.

“No, no, I feel partly uh, responsible. Considering, the uh, whole bond thing,” he says a little stiffly. He turns bodily away enough that I can’t really see his face through the gap in the stairwell now, just a slice of his back.

“But um… I would save the research for your home computer,” he says over his shoulder.

This whole bonding thing has me off kilter. It seems like everything I say or do is just a little too much. It’s like I don’t know how to be Cool Janice. Subdued, Unaffected, Perfectly Poised Janice. That's the only reason I end up blurting out, "Have any recommendations?"

Oh my god that's the exact opposite of being cool. I meant it to sound ironically flirty and a hundred percent joking. A squeak in my voice makes it err into genuine.

He lifts an eyebrow, and maybe it's the angle he's looking at me or his expression, but it makes my cheeks flare again. "...If you give me your personal email, I can send you some stuff."

"Just don't tell your mom you're sending me porn, ok? I won't be able to live down, even if I never meet her," I stage whisper through the railing bars, because I can't not keep trying to play it off.

He coughs. "It wasn't going to–, I mean, I would never–"

My face flushes an entirely new shade of red at Unhinged Janice's behavior, and I quickly escape back into the hallway.

6

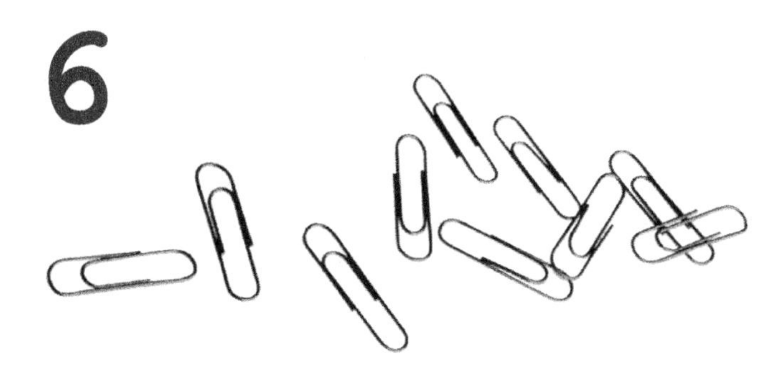

My heart doesn't flutter and my clit does not pulse awake when I get the email to set up the training appointment. Those parts don't start doubling down on those sensations in the minutes leading up to it either.

The next time I get to see Khent, he's sitting on the far end of the room like before.

We didn't tear each other's clothes off in the stairwell, when there was significantly less space between us. I try to remind myself that it's good to be cautious anyway.

Still, my heart does leap a little at how quickly he looks up when I come in. He looks back down at his stack of print-outs. The training questions and quiz.

I remind myself that I don't feel the need to start riding the seam of my pants to appease the endless, heightened need between my legs when I sit down across the room from him, as per MR's instructions about staying apart.

He attempts to slide a paper down the fifteen foot table, it makes it about two feet before the glossy stickiness of the table snags the page. He pulls it back to himself and tries it again, same result.

"I'll just make it work from this end of the table," he shrugs, giving me a sheepish smile. I do appreciate the effort he's putting into staying far enough apart from me.

"And here I was hoping you were going to make a paper airplane next," I quip, a little smile tugging at the corner of my mouth. I immediately chew that smile out of existence, in case he thought I was flirting.

Amusement touches Khent's features, but he lets the comment roll off.

He reads me some instructions on how to identify malicious email addresses and links, I just kind of sink into the sound of his voice, the warmth and depth of it. My mind starts absently spinning a fantasy about what it must be like to lean my head against his chest and feel the rumble of his voice while he reads something soothing out loud.

He pauses every now and then to ask if I have any questions, and I end up asking him to repeat and explain this in more detail just to hear him keep talking.

The way his hair looks like an interpretation of a tidal wave after he runs a hand through it isn't actually that cute, I tell myself. It's just the Blood Fever, I remind myself. It's not a real attraction.

At some point we move onto the quiz portion of this training session, and I probably should have focused more on the content of what he was saying, instead of the cavernous quality of his voice. Can you really blame me?

"Is it a good idea to mouse over a link to reveal its true destination?"

"Umm... yes?" I sound distracted. I am.

He scratches something onto the paper with a pen. "What should you do if you receive a suspicious email? The options are, A, share it with your coworkers. B, unplug your computer. C, don't open any links."

I watch Khent for a moment, as he glances up from the sheet and adjusts his glasses.

I kind of enjoyed that moment we had in the stairwell the other day. Not in a Blood Fever, mate-bondy way. Just in a normal, he's-not-so-bad kind of way. He's kind of fun, when he can't hide behind the impersonal nature of emailing.

“Unplugging the computer sounds reasonable,” I say, crossing my arms.

He frowns at me. “Seriously? The answer is right there. That’s the easiest question on it.”

“There doesn't seem to be anything wrong with unplugging it though,” I say, wondering how long it would take to tease that side out of him again.

“Can I get a virus from unplugging my computer, Khent?”

“You can do damage to your computer that way,” he says flatly, though he lifts an amused eyebrow.

My smile widens. I’ve got him. “Believe me, I know all the ways to damage a computer.”

The words come out of me almost in a purr, I sound so pleased with myself.

Khent goes very still for a moment. I don’t expect to hear him say, “Go on.”

“Let’s see. I used to let my cat sleep right up against my laptop’s vent,” I start, resting my chin in my hand, leaning just the slightest bit closer in the fifteen-foot gap between us. “The fan stopped turning, it was so clogged with fur.”

He winces briefly in sympathy for my personal laptop.

“And then I would sit it down on a big fuzzy blanket that shed a lot. I actually melted one of the components onto the motherboard that way.”

"You're evil," he says, shaking his head, but I can see the smile curling around his tusks and how hard he's trying to hold it back.

"You don't know the half of it," I grin.

He leans his chin into his palm, holding my gaze.

The conference room door opens suddenly, shattering whatever fragile wonder had been growing between us in that moment.

A water nymph pokes his head in. "Is this room open?"

"It was reserved," Khent answers quickly. "We're using it."

There's a bit of a crowd hanging outside the door, they have their lunches with them. I can smell the takeout from here.

The one leaning in the doorway glances up and down the wide, empty ocean of conference table between Khent and me. He looks skeptical.

"There's a smaller room open down the hall if you guys want to move to it," he says after a couple beats. "We couldn't fit everybody in that one for our lunch meeting."

His words hang in the air a moment.

He clearly expects us to accommodate him. In other circumstances, I wouldn't have minded doing so. But there's kind of a medical condition here.

Khent, despite being about as wide as a desk, seems to shrink in on himself a little as the water nymph looks to him. He ducks his head down, shakes a hand through his hair like it could buy some kind of time.

"We did reserve this room," Khent says hesitantly, like he's not really sure how to hold his ground on that.

"Yeah, but," the nymph makes a gesture to the emptiness of the room, scrunching up his scaly face, "Are you really using it?"

My eyes flick back and forth between the two, taking in their body language, a moment of clarity shifting into place.

I wonder if it's easier for Khent to work on the fourth floor, where the IT department has less people and more storage, the reduced foot traffic and passerby's, working on issues that have clear cut scripts. I don't think I've ever met a socially anxious Orc before.

"Yes, we are," I interrupt, raising my voice to take up the space that the nymph thinks is up for grabs, still keeping it on this side of polite. "Consider reserving it first, next time."

The nymph turns his head to me.

"You're interrupting my training," I say, keeping my tone assertive, though the way my blood heats up protectively nearly turns my voice aggressive. "Now, if you would please close the door."

The nymph pauses a moment, before sighing and obliging.

I turn my stare back to Khent when I'm sure we're alone. There's a sort of awe in his expression, dark green flush in his cheeks that sends a warmth up mine.

"I'll just, um. Mark your training complete," he stumbles to say, running a nervous hand through his hair again.

7

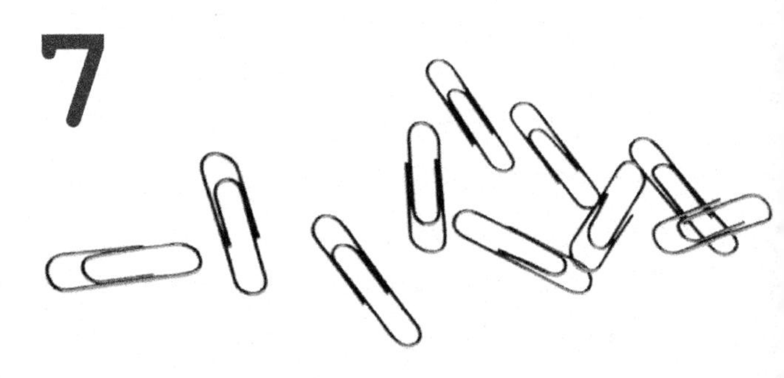

I didn't end up hearing from the IT Department for several days after that meeting.

I don't know if I was happy or not about that. I mean, as far as I could tell, that meant that no one was following up on my Not Safe for Work searches.

But it also meant I hadn't talked to Khent for several days.

Which was the idea. Getting as much space from him as possible was what Monsters Resources instructed. Eventually, my vulva would receive the message.

I tried working from home one day, but that was a bad idea in itself. With my personal laptop right there, wearing sweatpants, that post-it note with the Orc porn website and my vibrator a mere room away, well. I got very little done.

I think I watched that video I'd clicked on at work, the one with the claiming ritual, at least a dozen times. It did something different for me, made the fever feel not like burning up, but warm and cozy. Like I was lying in a sunbeam and soaking it up, instead of sweating in a summer-hot car.

In the claiming ritual video it looked like, in the most polite of terms, there was a somewhat intense penetration and exchange of body fluids. There was some kind of oil involved, made of some unspecified herbs mashed up until they were liquid. It moved like oil but looked like ink in the bottle. It was shinier than anything else when it was used, from where it was used like lube and where it was swirled in shapes and spread along the skin.

And there was a lot of spreading.

At first I insisted to myself that I was rewatching how this whole mating ritual thing was done so that I could assure myself I hadn't done anything similar with Khent that time in my office.

Of course, that excuse wore out when I realized I pretty much had the video memorized.

I kind of wanted to call Khent and ask questions. Were the herbs or oil used in the ritual the sticking point of the whole mating thing? Also like, how was his day going?

Then again, I couldn't really do that without making things weird again, realistically.

I mean, it wasn't just the Blood Fever making me want to talk to Khent. We were in the same boat, I didn't have anyone else to complain about how being constantly, unendingly horny was wreaking havoc on my sleep schedule. Or how it made my legs weirdly sore from how they were constantly tensing up. I mean, what kind of guy doesn't email you after he mate-bonds with you? Even though he technically already did.

So nature, and uh, Unhinged Janice, She Who Destroys Computers, find a way.

I did not succeed in melting my computer, not even after running every program I had on the computer at the same time for an hour or so. But the screen started flickering just after I opened a few hefty spreadsheets, and when I came back to it after lunch, the screen wouldn't turn on. I had my excuse to call the IT Department.

"Try turning it off and on again," he says over the phone.

Since I'm back in my office, whenever he speaks, I squeeze my knees together and shift my hips in my chair. Above the desk line at least, I'm pretending the sound of his voice hasn't wet my panties instantly. I brought more underwear to work, because at least I'm now ready for this. I also brought a little cooler full of ice packs, so that I could make it through meetings without trying to hump my chair.

"No, no don't give me that, I'm not restarting it again," I pull off my glasses and put the end of the temple between my teeth.

"Did you already try restarting?"

"...No," I mumble a bit sheepishly. I push the receiver away from my face as I grumble, "That's what the IT guys say to trick you into forgetting what the actual problem was."

"Humor me," he says, his voice pure patience. His voice is soothing mental itches I didn't know I had. It's deep and complex and I don't think I've ever listened this closely just to the sound of someone's voice before.

Blood Fever is one hell of a drug.

I harrumph as loudly as possible into the receiver so that there's no mistaking my displeasure. I've been onto these IT guys and their quick fix solutions that give you the runaround.

"It's still doing the thing," I snap, perhaps a little too triumphantly, when the screen flickers through the start up.

Khent hums a little on the other end of the line, a note of amusement. "That's not a good thing."

"Well. I guess that means it's just broken, right?" I twirl the office desk phone's chunky wire cord around my finger a moment, and stop myself just before I offer to bring the laptop down to IT myself.

As good as the plan cooked up by my nethers sounds right now, it would be entirely counterproductive. I just wanted to chat for some solidarity or something. Not to announce my impending arrival so we could find a storage closet to get to know each other in.

"There's something else we can try," Khent offers after a few moments, and it does take me a second to remember what he means about my computer. Not like, positions or locations.

I put him on speaker phone, just to get the intimate hush of his voice out of my ear.

"Alright, what do I do?"

"Turn it off."

"AGAIN?"

"And then unplug the laptop."

I grumble and do as he says, wondering if this is all the IT guys do every day. "Ok."

"And then flip it over, there should be a slider to release the battery, so you can remove it."

The slider takes a moment to open, but then I'm holding the battery in my hand. It's heavy, and about as wide as the laptop. "Ok, now what?"

"Shake out all those electrons."

"Your credentials are getting less believable by the second," I mutter. That can't be real. That sounds so unsciencey. Is he pulling my leg, or do I actually need to do that?

Instead of just asking for clarification, I say, “I think you’re just enjoying telling me what to do.”

He just chuckles. “I have been known to abuse my power.”

A beat goes by, and I do end up shaking the battery, just in case. Then I feel like an idiot and put it down.

“What do I do next?”

“Now we just let it sit for a minute,” he answers simply.

“We just sit here?”

“For a minute.”

A few seconds of silence stretch before us. Somehow the quiet is what makes me squirm. It's just the sound of his breath and mine. It's comfortable, even though the memory of the other day lingers over our interactions.

I kind of want to apologize for making this whole mate bonding dilemma harder than it already is. But that apology has a number of other struck through thoughts that I didn’t get to first, about the broken nose and broken glasses, and honestly anything else I might have broken at this point.

“I gotta apologize again,” he says, like he’s thinking all the same things I was.

“Not again, you don't,” I return quickly, because he's beating me in the apologies department and leaving me in the dust.

“I have to,” he says, concern in his voice. “I mean, I understand the whole mate bonding thing is highly unusual to humans–”

“Oh, please. This is by no means the worst thing to happen to me at work,” I scoff, really just to get him to stop worrying about the comfort level of humans. It’s also kind of an attempt to get him to stop apologizing all the time. Really, I need him to stop.

“...What was?” Khent asks after a beat.

I probably should have anticipated him asking me that, I did put it out there. But my arms close around my chest and I have to stop myself from reactively turning away, the phone cord wrapping around my shoulder with the movement of my swivel chair.

“It was, uh, at the last company I worked at,” I say, my voice falling into a softer register, almost hushed. It's not a secret, but it's not something I exactly want to think about.

Sometimes I tell the story of my biggest dating mistake at parties or among friends, sometimes as my bid to win some verbal ‘Dated the World's Biggest Asshole’ contest. It’s usually a third glass of wine kind of story. Ultimately, I tell it to make people laugh, to gasp and say 'oh my god, what a dick'.

“I dated one of my coworkers for a while,” I admit out loud and cringe a little, the words like admitting some huge misstep. Still, I can't fault myself for choosing that relationship, I was younger and it had been exciting precisely because it was the wrong choice. “We were in the same department. At first that made it easy for us to talk to each other, we bonded over complaining about the same things at our job.”

Khent hums a little, a note of safeness that nudges me along.

I sit forward and tap my fingers on the desk. As much as revealing this in a plain, non-joking way makes me want to curl into a ball of shame, I want to see him. I want to watch his expression, to try to read his thoughts from his posture. But I also know that would be a mistake. We shouldn’t be trying to get to know each other any better.

“But he was a bit competitive with me. If our boss told me I did a good job on something, he would take it like some kind of personal insult. One day, our boss hinted that I was due for a promotion. And James– well. My ex went and told our friends that I had slept with the boss to get it. And when I confronted him about it, he said it was a joke. Just a joke.”

This is the part where my voice shakes a little as I tell it. In the quiet of my office, confessing into the receiver, it's much more evident than at parties, where my friends usually explode into outrage and giggle madly over another round of drinks.

I don't know what I want Khent to say in response to this. All I know is I hope maybe someone like him would understand. Maybe he'll see how these memories hang over me and steer me.

At worst, maybe he'll laugh.

“He said this while you were still dating?” Khent asks, and it strikes me as odd.

It's not something I had ever really considered. Would it have made more sense if it had happened after we had broken up?

“Yeah, we were still dating at the time. I mean, not long after. Maybe he thought he could tell everyone this hilarious joke of his and that I would just be ok with it. And when we had to sort our shit out with HR, it came up, and there was a whole investigation into whether or not I had actually slept with my boss in exchange for the promotion. And at the end of it all, well. Companies don't really care about you. They care about not getting sued for the indiscretions of their other employees.”

I didn't tell it right. There wasn't humor or theatrics in my voice like there usually was.

I realize I'm clutching myself a little too tight, the quiet anger I keep at the back of my throat is bared on my teeth, dripping venom into my tone. The line is utterly silent. For a fearful heartbeat, I wonder if I've scared Khent off.

"Needless to say, I didn't get promoted," I ramble on in the face of Khent's quiet, injecting some upbeat casualness into my tone. That is the punchline to this story, after all. "I figured if I got a job at Evil Inc., then at least they would be transparent about their priorities."

"He should have – *fuck*."

I don't think I've ever heard an Orc swear quietly before, like he's trying to smother the word. The effect of it undoes some of the knot in my chest.

I don't think I could emotionally withstand Khent being protective of me, even if it's a year too late. I can live with being horny, but being cared about might cross a line. There's HR paperwork we would need to file for that.

"Um, when do I put the battery back in?" I mumble, hoping we can bury the subject with another one.

"Ah. Yeah, you can put it back in and turn it on," he says, some remnants of emotion still in his voice. Clearly he hadn't expected to shift gears like that.

"Oh. It works fine now," I say, as the screen lights up.

"Don't sound so thrilled," Khent chuckles through the phone.

I throw a sheepish look at my keyboard.

"It's called power cycling. Try it next time this happens."

"Oh, but then I wouldn't get to annoy you about it," I tease. I am starting to enjoy these little chats. Not because of the bond or anything, it's just nice to have someone new to talk to.

He gives a soft laugh in response, and almost reflexively, I ask, "So… how are you doing with all this?"

A beat goes by before he replies. "Uh… you want the real answer?"

I scoff and sputter a moment, probably turning a bright, vivid red to complement his earthy green. Ok, maybe that's a Not So Safe For Work kind of question. Maybe I want to know, maybe it's not just because he's the only person I know also going through this.

"I just meant, um, do you feel like it's starting to clear up for you? Yet?"

I twist the phone's cord between my fingers a little too tight, and I'm kind of worried he'll say he's just about gotten over his fever. The thought makes my heart sink a little. Because if he's recovered just fine, then we won't have any reason to talk to each other anymore.

And that does make me sad.

I don't know why. Maybe this whole ordeal inflated my ego with the thought that someone could just be openly, earnestly and irrevocably in love with me. And that it could be a guy as nice and sweet (and broad, let's be real) as Khent.

Maybe I don't want him to be done with all this because I just don't want to be the only one feeling this. Because it really has not changed at all for me. It's starting to feel like I'm going to be like this forever.

"Uh, a bit, maybe," he says, and my heart sinks a little further.

"Really?" I bite my mouth closed to keep from immediately asking for more details.

"Most likely because I've been visiting this sort of holistic place in my neighborhood," he says, and my heart trampolines back up into my chest, possibly my throat.

I should be more excited at the prospect of getting over all this than I am at the thought that our accidental mating bond isn't just fading away on its own for him.

I nod quickly even though he can't see me. "Do you think– I mean, could I give that a try? Would that be weird or a bad idea?"

"Well, I'm not your doctor, clearly," he goes on, like the coolest cucumber, like we're not discussing how to stem the tide of Blood Fever. "But I've found it beneficial."

"And it's not like medicines that have yet to be tested on humans that could have weird side effects, right?"

I can hear his chair creak as he leans back in it, considering my question. "I've seen humans and all kinds of monsters go. Usually for the novelty of the experience, less for medical needs."

My nails are between my teeth like a conduit for the thoughts turning over in my brain. I don't really want to go on my own, like I'll be perceived as some weirdo human tourist.

He pauses a moment as he gathers a breath. That hint of a smile in his voice deepens as he suggests, "...I've got a coupon for two, if you like."

Fuck. He knows the way I think. I feel weirdly soft and melty and warm under my bra, and that's a new symptom of horniness for me. Maybe we're accidentally mate bonded or whatever, but I really like that he seems to know me, that he sees the little details that would go unnoticed by someone who cared a little less.

I stop short of telling him that of all people to get cosmically tangled up with, I'm glad it was him. That might be a little too genuine an emotion to have on company time.

8

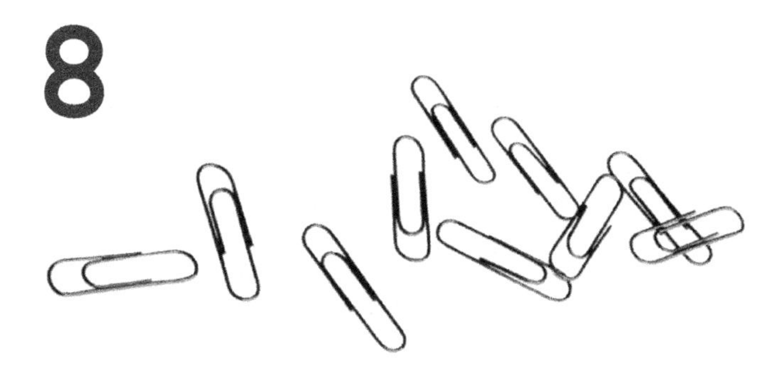

The rest of the work day, I could barely think about anything but my not-date with Khent.

Because it wasn't a date.

It was more like after work drinks with some coworkers, totally platonic, a hundred percent about the group morale and departmental bonding. Except that it was just the two of us. And it would be inter-departmental. And there would be no bonding.

I was looking forward to it because I was ready to not look at my vibrator for a week. Maybe two weeks. To not constantly wonder if I was coming down with a regular human fever, or if it was just another flare up of the Blood Fever whenever my skin started to heat.

I'd thought perhaps he was just coping with the Blood Fever better, but this was totally the reason why. And if it worked on me too, then maybe getting through this would be a lot easier.

Clearly whatever these holistic practices were, they worked. As far as I could tell, Khent didn't seem nearly as affected by the Blood Fever as I was. At least, for as much as I was constantly pressing my thighs together, I hadn't noticed him strategically angling a hard-on away from me. Which maybe was something I might have been on the lookout for after that video. Just professional curiosity.

After a few short emails (to my personal address, not my work one) we decided to meet in the lobby. I pressed the elevator button maybe a dozen times on the way down.

We took separate cars, of course, with me following him from the more metropolitan part of the city, to a part that was surprisingly surrounded by lush green park land.

The name of the place is in Orcish calligraphy, sort of blocky and sweepy at the same time. I think in a college ceramics elective I learned something about how Orcish calligraphy is done with a square of dyed clay repeatedly dipped into an herbal tea between letter strokes. We'd done a little unit on kneading the dye into the clay and trying to inscribe our badly made creations with the technique, but it was surprisingly difficult to manage.

Khent was waiting outside as I walked up the building steps. He held the door for me, and Evil Overlord, if that didn't make me shiver and warm again. No matter, this would soon be easier. There would be no more clutching my hands to myself to avoid climbing Khent like a tree. Or really, more like a boulder. He was definitely more boulder shaped.

As soon as we stepped inside, the quiet of the building washed over us. It was mildly humid and warmer than it was outside.

"Do you think I could write this off as a work expense?" I whisper to Khent, standing in line at the - spa? Sauna? Spauna? "What's this place called?"

He chuckles low in his throat a moment. "You couldn't pronounce it."

"Thanks for the vote of confidence."

Whatever. I'm still fully prepared to save the receipt, send a copy of it to the Accounting department, and CC Gwen in the email.

Of course, being near Khent in line is its own little mistake. Maybe I should have waited by the door or one of the windows, but I'll be damned if I let him pay for my half.

Apparently, I'm vibrating obviously enough that he feels the need to put a hand on the top of my head to stop it, like I'm an antique alarm clock or something that would dance off the bedside table with my fidgety energy.

I make a point of staring at the fingertips resting just over my forehead. Khent rolls his eyes and after a moment, he transfers his hand to just resting on my shoulder. If someone looked at us, they would just see a couple casually, almost boringly embraced while waiting in line.

My chest tightens for a moment. It's been a while since I had that kind of relationship. Wouldn't it be nice to be so safe it’s almost boring? To not be on guard all the time?

The tension I've been holding in my back melts momentarily, or maybe it slips, and then my shoulder is falling into Khent's side.

I’m as still as I possibly can be against him.

I barely pay attention to the transaction at the counter, I honestly don’t hear much, if anything the harpy behind the counter says. I nod along as if I do.

Only when it’s over, I separate myself from him. We follow an Orc woman down a hallway. Normally Khent’s stride could easily outpace me, but he slows himself to walk beside me.

She stops in front of a pair of doors to two different rooms, and opens both of them.

“It’s set up already. There’s a bell if you need anything else, but otherwise, you have the full hour,” she says more to Khent than me, probably because I’m peering around her to see what's inside.

For a few feet, it's just a normal room, with regular tile and some shelves. Further in, the light is softer, from a ceiling that is nearly obscured with steam billowing down. The walls and floor seem carpeted almost entirely in lichen and shaggy moss. There's a low bed that looks like it's been carved from stone.

"Thanks," Khent nods. He glances at me, and I nod vigorously. I'm ready. I cannot wait to feel totally relaxed and rejuvenated and not horny.

Khent's mouth tips to the side in an unsure smile. We kind of awkwardly wave at one another and go into each room separately, closing the doors behind us.

I look around at the room before me once I'm alone. Lichen is still where it was before. I look to the shelf beside me, and kick off my shoes, some sensible flats have finally stopped cutting the back of my heels open. I stick them in the cubby.

I take in the room for a few more minutes, as it dawns on me I have no idea what to do. I grumble at myself for not thinking to ask Khent more info about these holistic practices he's been doing.

I open the door and gingerly step across the cold slate floors to Khent's door. I only just took off my shoes a second ago, so it doesn't really occur to me to knock.

My eyes find the white towel being unfolded first, then separate the form of the entirely green, entirely bare Orc from the lichen behind him.

Brain short circuits.

Oh, Overlord. Nudity.

Close the door, quick quick quick.

I manage that much, but I'm still on the wrong side.

"Janice?"

Look away. Look down.

My eyes snag on his cock before I force them to the ground. My cheeks scald.

I have a number of thoughts, most of them about the mere logistics of him fitting inside me that I immediately stamp down. I do think I could manage it, maybe.

"If I'd known we were supposed to undress, maybe I would have knocked," I stammer out.

So the Orc pornstar I'd been ogling before was not an outlier, ok, that's something new. You learn something every day. Knowledge is amazing.

"Maybe you would have knocked?" Khent repeats in disbelief, and stifles a snort. "What are the odds on that maybe, like a 50-50? 60-40?"

"I'll get those numbers on your desk by tomorrow," I sigh, scrubbing my hands over my face, and peeking through my fingers. He has the towel wrapped around his waist now, fastened at his hip.

With herculean effort, I bring my eyes up to his face.

"I think that answers my question though," I nod, and duck out of the room. Once safely back in my little room, I take my clothes off and pile them on the shelf. The towel is big enough to wrap around me twice, and about as long as a dress on me.

Man, I want towels like these. All my towels at home are too short to wrap around me even once.

I swear I'm just hypnotized by the soft luxuriousness of these towels, and that's why my mind wanders off into a scenario where I come here more often with Khent.

I pinch myself. *No, don't think like that. That's just the Blood Fever talking.*

After I'm done admiring the size of these towels, it occurs to me that I still super do not know what I'm supposed to be doing in here.

This time when I shuffle to Khent's door, I knock.

"Yeah?"

"It's me again," I call through the door.

"More questions?"

I scoot through the door and the image that greets me nearly knocks me over, I stumble back against the door as it shuts.

Khent is – all of his green glory, sitting down on that mossy stone stool. His knees splayed wide, the towel draped over them making me forget why I came in here.

The humidity in the room is starting to condensate on his skin. His shoulders are just massive.

"I don't know what I'm doing in there," I confess after a few minutes.

"You didn't read the links I sent you?"

"I was in meetings till the end of my day," I lie, and I'm sure he sees right through it. I shake my head quickly. "Can you show me what to do? And then, I promise I'll go back into my room, and I won't bother you again. I swear."

I feel like everything I say to Khent is dipped in defensiveness, but when I look at him, the openness of his posture, his expression, I wonder why I felt the need at all. He looks even a little happy that I'm here, asking him this.

"I'll show you."

"You will?"

"Sure."

The moss that carpets the floor is soft and damp underfoot as I cross to sit on the stone slab. It's probably a good thing the towel wraps around me twice so he definitely can't see the way my nipples harden when I step closer to him.

My hand will probably have terry cloth imprinted on it by the time I'm back in my room and I can stop clutching the knot closed like it's my sole lifeline.

Khent pauses by an arrangement of stones that, to me, had mostly blended in with the rest of the room's pocket of nature.

I hadn't seen the little waterfall weaving between the stones of that panel the back wall, the water pooling in a small basin. As I step nearer to it, I can feel how it's the source of most of the warmth in this room.

He picks up a little vial from a shelf, unscrewing the top. He's clearly well versed in what one's supposed to do in this room.

From the vial, he drops a little dark colored oil on a heated metal disk, a small tuft of vapor blooms off from it.

There's so little of it used, but taking in a breath of it is amazing. It's less like a smell and more like a sensation. Like being rolled up in fresh sheets still warm from the dryer. There's a hint of something almost musky.

I guess I should do the same things he's doing? So I reach for it as well.

"You're don't want to touch that," Khent says abruptly, pulling me from my thoughts as well as physically tugging me back. He sweeps me back a few steps like it was dangerous.

"I wasn't going to touch the hot plate," I protest, getting my bearings back after that dizzying swoosh.

"Not that, the oil," he says, and my eyes fall back on the incense smelling stuff. Turning away from me, he explains, "It's, uh, usually used in mating rituals."

"That stuff they draw on each other's faces with?" I blurt out. Jeez, isn't it dangerous to keep that in here? Then again, I did come in here on my own.

He pauses and turns back around to me, raising an eyebrow as if to prompt how I knew that.

I cross my arms. "I wasn't just watching porn at work, y'know."

"No, just romantic porn," he snorts. It doesn't escape my notice that he considers porn that includes a mating ritual romantic. I guess if he grew up on it, he would.

"Well, it's weird to watch porn when it doesn't have a plot!" I return, only to realize half a second later I'm digging a deeper grave for myself. I lock my teeth together and straighten my spine. No, I'm not going to act like that's a weird thing to prefer. "At least a little bit of emotional connection is important to me."

"You know, you can stop telling me about your preferences in pornography at any moment you feel like it," he says, though there's a teasing undercurrent in his tone. I can see the shy smile tugging at his tusks.

I want more of that smile.

“Well, if it doesn't end in a creampie then it's not worth my time either,” I announce, and it's fully worth it for the expression that crosses his face as he tries not to laugh.

“Emotional connections and creampies. Noted,” Khent sighs, burying his face in his hands. He doesn't completely hide the dark green flush in his cheeks.

I turn my attention back to the heated metal with the oil to give him a breath, and because it snags my curiosity again.

After a few moments, he says, like that whole dirty tangent didn't just occur, “Heating a drop or two of that can help take the edge off some of the Blood Fever symptoms.”

“Oh. Do you think I could take some home?”

“They probably sell little bottles of it at the front desk.”

I nod, taking that in. I could put together a little hot plate or something at my desk that would simulate this. Maybe that would make all this a lot easier.

Of course, I'm not totally sure it's doing anything to abate the feelings I'm having right now.

My eyes draw to the way sweat is already gathering on his skin. I’m overly aware of my tongue and how it’s still just in my mouth. “And that’s how you’ve been relaxing these last few days?”

He shrugs. “I’ve definitely found it to work a reasonable amount. But if you listen to your matriarch too much, she’s bound to tell you it cures everything from poison ivy to broken bones."

I nod, and a small laugh escapes me.

"My grandma used to make me put yogurt on my sunburns. I think I totally trusted her faith in that working until a few years ago."

The steam is gathering on his glasses, and he pushes them up on top of his head as he nods. It feels a little like permission to stare unabashedly into his dark brown eyes. I wonder how bad his eyesight is without them, if I just become a blur to him, or if he can still see where I'm staring.

I stare too long. It's gotta be obvious after a minute.

I quickly turn back to the heated stone, scooping up a bowl full of water to add more steam to the room.

"...So, am I doing this right yet? Just sit here in the steam? Or would your matriarch tell me I'm doing it wrong?"

I look from him to the waterfall behind him a couple times to check his expression without staring too long again.

He chews the corner of his mouth as he watches me flip back and forth. "It does work better if you relax."

"RELAX?" I repeat, and maybe it comes out a little strangled. I swallow and nod. "Ok. How do you usually relax?"

He tilts his head to what I had mistaken for a shallow pool earlier. From here, it does seem more like a bathing spring.

Gulp.

9

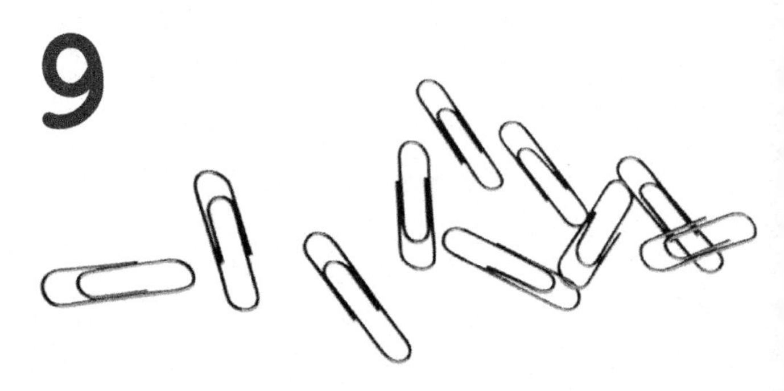

The pit of anxiousness in my stomach urges me to say 'You first' in regards to the pool, and then bolt out of the room the moment he's not looking directly at me, and yell something about getting more of that herbal oil stuff over my shoulder.

It would be a smart decision, to remove myself from temptations now that I know what I should be doing.

I look at Khent and the sheen of sweat on his skin and it melts away.

I have not been making smart decisions.

Approaching the pool, I dip a toe in. The water is warm, like everything in here. Only I'm not so much worried about the temperature, but what might happen in it.

I take a step into the pool, aiming for the little stone stairs that draw you in. My foot plunges into the water much further down than I anticipated.

Khent's hand catches mine and balances me as I wobble and nearly slip. The water nearly comes up to my knee, my other hand is bunching up the luxuriously huge towel to keep it from getting wet.

I stand there uncertainly a moment, clutching Khent and the towel.

Clearly everything here is tailored to a differently sized clientele. I feel like a goddamn gnome. The towels I was daydreaming about somehow masterfully folding into a shape that would fit into my purse so I could bring one home, have suddenly become a death trap. If I try to take a soak in this hot spring with a big fluffy towel the size of a bedsheet, it's going to absorb all the water instantly and be impossible to move in. It'll pull me down into the bottom.

I glance back at Khent, whose head is turned away just enough to give me some semblance of privacy.

Does it really matter if I'm naked in front of him if he's already eaten me out?

I wrestle with the towel a moment, one handedly tugging it off and trying to toss it aside without it getting too wet.

The humidity hits my skin and makes me all too aware of how alone I am with Khent. I take another step in and let go of his hand. I sit down on the first step, and the water comes up to my collarbone.

I take a moment trying to figure out how to sit in a way that hides my bits, like some kind of tasteful sculpture and not a NSFW bonding activity. I settle for propping my elbow on my knee to censor my nipples. Good enough.

"Relaxing. Like this?"

"In whatever way you feel best," he says, his voice a soft rumble.

Another ounce of tension seeps into my jaw in at the vagueness of his words. I need clearer instructions, dammit.

I barely relax on my days off. I mean, how does anyone relax in late-stage evil empiricism? You work all week, then maybe get a couple of chores and enough laundry done on the weekends to survive another few days. I'm always trying to out-work the system, like if I can just get up early enough I'll somehow find a secret stash of hours to use, instead of just stealing sleep from my body. There's the sound of another towel falling to the ground and it takes everything in me not to whip around and watch. No, I'm going to try to afford Khent the same professional courtesy he just showed me. Because we're professionals. And coworkers.

The one thing I think this place has going for it is that there's so many sensations from the heat and humidity and the water, that I can almost tune out the feeling of my cunt aching to be touched.

At least, until I look at Khent again.

A small wave brushes past me. Khent enters the pool and makes himself comfortable on the step next to me.

Don't look into the water. Don't look. Don't look.

My eyes dip down. The water quickly distorts anything more than a couple inches down out of view. Damn.

Sitting beside me, he still towers over me, but it feels a little less stilted between us as he takes on a relaxed pose. The way the water laps at his abdomen and leaves little droplets behind makes me want to lick them off of him.

I swallow and try to school my face into something less blatantly obviously ogling. I glance back at the heated stones he had poured the tea over before. "Can you go through the steps with me again?"

He gives me a look that I can't parse. What, am I wasting his hour? I'll find him another coupon or something.

"I just— I don't know what I'm supposed to be doing in here and I don't want to do it wrong and then this doesn't work, you know?"

"Mate-bonding is really all that much of an inconvenience for you?" His face sort of pinches even as he says that word, *inconvenience*.

I can't stop the way my face falls at his question. I'm ashamed that I haven't been better at hiding that. He's been so nice and understanding through this whole mess. I don't want to keep trampling on cultural norms the public education system never really taught me about. I don't want to hurt him.

Instead, I curl my legs up to my chest and hug my arms around myself. "It's just– it's different. It's such a sudden attachment and I– I've always been self-sufficient, y'know? You know what it's like, being like that."

"Can't say I do," he sighs. That's where we differ, I guess.

I look away. We're an odd pair. We never would have gotten together on our own, it only happened because of a mistake that occurred when we crossed paths.

I don't really register the way the water ripples with Khent's movements as he leans out of the water, the sound of a ceramic jar scraping across the stone.

"Here," Khent says, drawing my attention. He's unscrewed the lid of some jar, and holds out a hand.

I offer him mine, raising an eyebrow. "That also some salve for relaxing?"

"It's just plain massage oil." He takes a gentle hold of my wrist. With his other hand he starts to spread the oil all the way up my arm. He starts to massage the oil into my skin, the circular motion of it easing the tension from my muscles.

"I've always been surrounded by attachments," he says, the words quiet as the water lapping at the stones. "It's hard to be a loner in Orc communities, there's always someone that needs you, family or friends. Sometimes it's too much to keep up with. But I guess it always made me look forward to having this kind of…attachment."

I hum a note of amusement. He's using the word I did, but it sounds less clinical coming from him.

He's worked his way to my shoulder. This stuff is amazing. I don't know why we started with the tea on the hot stone when this was an option.

"It's someone who's on your side, on your wavelength. When you can't keep up with life, they're there to help you."

"I guess. I haven't had much luck finding someone like that. I mean, none of my exes ever did the dishes," I say. It's half a joke, mostly true.

"You don't believe there's someone out there that completes you?"

"I— well," I choke on my words backtracking. I doubt there's anyone out there willing to put up with my bullshit. To date, no one has. I just knock heads with everyone. But I'm going to try not to put my foot in my mouth.

"I believe there's someone out there that completes *you*," I try, and that much is genuine. I really hope there's someone out there that deserves Khent, as kind and patient as he is. And if his soul-mate isn't totally worthy of him, well, I guess I'm going to beat her up or something.

"I've never really been much for taking initiative. I've been told I'm conflict avoidant," he says, a sort of ponderous tone that suggests he's given this a lot of thought. He's probably spent his whole life wondering what the person who completes him would be like.

That solidifies it in my mind. I will totally take this bitch to the woodshed if she even thinks about not being good enough for him.

"But I've always admired people who take charge and stand up for themselves," he shrugs.

I imagine there's a lot of Orc women like that. I get lost in thinking about some other woman completing Khent. I realize after a moment my heart is beating a little too fast.

He lets go of my arm that's closest to him, and I feel weirdly unbalanced. The one side of me is soothed and unwound, and the other side is still tightly coiled with all the stress I've been carrying around.

I scoot up on my ankle to try to pivot around so he has access to my other arm, but that has me kneeling on the step and my knees don't like it.

I think about it for all of ten seconds. I mean, we're naked in a hot spring together. How much worse is it to sit on his lap?

It's definitely my best decision in a while. The relief my body feels at the contact, my bare ass against his thighs, it's doing much more for me than the steam bath did.

If Khent is surprised by the boldness of my actions, he doesn't voice it.

I have to keep talking or I'm going to keep thinking about what sitting in his lap means. "That's kind of the part of the whole soul mates thing that doesn't click with me. I'm complete all by myself, y'know? There isn't some incomplete half of me wandering around out there that I'm waiting for."

Khent hums, a deep rumbly sound that reverberates up through where my ass meets his thigh into my core. Maybe that's just my imagination, or wishful thinking. He sounds contemplative, nonetheless.

"I can see how people take issue with the way a lot of people talk about it. It does make romantic love sound like the end-all, be-all," he says after a while, his hands taking to working the oil into my other shoulder, down my arm. "But whatever language it gets couched in, or however people try to explain it, I think at the core of it all, it's just trying to describe someone whose presence makes you happy."

I twist around to look at him, I have to lean back against his chest just to balance myself. I think he's massaged his way past my muscles into my…feelings? Ick.

Whoever buys into stereotypes about Orcs being all grunts and no vocab clearly never met Khent. He's soft spoken with an insightful gravity in the way he speaks, like he's given a lot of thought and care to what he says.

He looks at me, my head against his shoulder, and his face softens. I wonder how well he can see me without his glasses. "You don't believe someone can make everything better, just by being there?"

The way I feel sitting in his lap, I would believe he could make my day better just by touching me. World peace would be achieved instantly if I had his cock in me.

"I don't—" I say, the words making me aware of how deeply I'm breathing. "I don't know."

The way he sounds when he talks about it makes me want to believe it. I don't think I have it in me to believe so genuinely in something as uncynical as that. But I want that kind of feeling he's talking about. Just leaning against him makes all my worries about work and life slip away.

It's not fair of me to want that much from Khent. I'd be taking advantage of his belief in this whole soul mates by Blood Fever thing if I just gave into it.

I shake my head, as if I could fling that thought out of my head like flinging droplets from my hair. Am I an asshole if I keep giving in to this?

I look at Khent, desperate to ask if the steam bath or the hot spring is working for him. Because I'm not convinced it's doing anything for me. But if I ask if it's working yet, he's just going to think I'm so inconvenienced by our bonding.

"Is– am I feeling all this because I'm right next to you?" I ask, making a sort of vague gesture that doesn't really illustrate my point.

Khent raises his eyebrows, a mixture of surprise and concern in his face, probably at how badly I'm expressing myself. "Sorry?"

"I don't know how to explain that being this close to you has made everything the Blood Fever is making me feel somehow better and worse at the same time–" I catch the way Khent's cheeks turn a darker green, flushing. "I think if I get out of your lap, my vagina is going to implode in on itself in horniness."

"Oh," he says "I don't know. I've never been in a situation like this before."

A moment passes, he continues to rub my shoulders. The rest of my body might be content to melt into his massive hands, but my cunt has yet to stop upping the ante.

"Maybe you can–" he turns his head away so fully his body turns too. He seems to forget I'm in his lap and he's taking me with him. "If you need to take care of yourself–"

He doesn't finish the offer, like the thought is too much to suggest. Like it doesn't merit the effort it takes to say.

I can feel his heart pounding through his chest to mine.

Wondering distantly if I care about holding him at arm's length anymore, I slip my hand between my thighs. I bite down on my lip as I find my clit, the sensation is needed, so wanted.

The relief I felt starts to crumble into need-want-need-please again. I wiggle a little, trying to scrape back that feeling. It works for a second before it falls back into craving.

His cock stiffens and brushes past my thighs in the water, the concave tip poking out of the surface. My mouth waters a little at the sight of the twin slits within the head. I can't take my eyes off him. It's kind of nice to know I'm not the only one affected.

"I want you to touch me," I beg, and I don't have it in me to be ashamed of how desperate I sound. Masturbating in his lap with him just wanting to touch me, but can't, is its own entirely appealing thought, but it needs to wait for an occasion when I can find a little more self-control.

Slowly, his hands draw up my thighs up my stomach to my breasts, still continuing to massage. Even though his hands are giant against me, his touch is staggeringly gentle. I want to be entirely wrapped up in this feeling. The brush of the pad of his fingertips against my nipples makes me want so much more.

I turn around, straddling him to the best of my ability. My mouth falls on his without even a thought.

Kissing Khent does something for my mind, the way taking a deep breath of cool air feels to my lungs. I pull back, breaking the kiss and remember I was trying not to do this. I can't give in to my body, this fever.

"Khent, but we shouldn't, right?" I say, even as my hips roll against him, his thick, heavy cock trapped between us. My hands are in his hair, and before I think about it, I pull myself up on my knees, as high as I can go. I find his cock, my hand stroking its incredible thickness, unable to fully circle around it. I'm doing the mental math, realizing that in order for his cockhead to peak above the water means that what I glimpsed before he was hard isn't lining up.

Evil Overlord, how is it possible that his cock was already huge to begin with *and* he's a grower??

I position the tip at my entrance. I know I can't. I shouldn't. We've been working so hard to get through this Blood Fever and just let the bond fade away. This is just going to make us need to start over again.

And besides, it might not even be physically possible.

"Then we should stop," he says, though nothing in his voice sounds like he agrees.

"Maybe, maybe just the tip," I say. I don't know enough about how mate-bonding and Blood Fever work to make that assumption, but my body is willing to run with that theory. "Maybe just a little bit is ok."

His hand curls around his cock, covering mine. He drags the tips back and forth through my pussy, teasing, torturing.

I almost whine in frustration, and move my hips, sinking down the smallest amounts to take him inside me. Even the first inch or so stretches my cunt to its capacity. It's wholly possible even just the tip is going to be too much for me.

I wonder distantly if my health insurance covers being eviscerated by Orc cock.

He nods, and his massive hands cup my ass, supporting my weight.

I rock my hips, gasping with every inch I'm slowly taking inside me. I'm going to have to make peace with the fact I'm just physically not going to be able to take all of him. Eventually.

I can see the way this is teasing him, the color in his cheeks and the strained cords in his neck. He's holding back while I work myself open.

I'm taking in more than the tip, sinking down a little too ambitiously with each thrust. Each time I nearly cry out from pushing myself too much, but my body adjusts after a few moments and craves more.

At least from what I can tell, I think he's a little more than halfway inside me, and that may truly be my limit. I should stop before this sends me to the ER.

"Maybe I could be there for you," he says, suddenly, snapping my thoughts away from death by dicking to something equally dangerous. Tenderness.

"What?"

"When you need someone to be on your side, or when you just need someone there."

That's not fair. He can't say that, not while I'm supernaturally horny and balanced on the tip of his dick, not when he's soothed every knot of tension out of my body and I just want to melt into his arms and kiss him again.

I look at him and try to find the words to tell him how completely unfair a suggestion that is. His expression stops me. I can see he actually wants that.

Maybe I want that too.

"Just, just a little," I manage to say.

Finally, he starts to roll his hips, pushing in and out of me, working more and more in. It's simultaneously too much and everything my body has been craving since that first incident.

He lifts me out of the water, rolling us over onto the soft mossy ground to continue to rut into me. I lift my hips to meet his rhythm, each time nearly enough to push me over into oblivion. More than once I lose my sense of self to the mere sensation of it all.

"It's– it's kind of been a while," he says, bringing my attention back to the moment. "Since I've been with anyone. Uh, sexually."

I kind of blink at him. Did he forget the encounter in my office? Either he's not making sense, or his dick has drained my brain power. He usually makes sense so I'm willing to believe the second option. "What?"

"I'm not going to last very long," he grunts, glancing away from me as he slows his thrusts.

My brain is so drenched in the endorphins, it takes me a few moments to realize what he's getting at.

"I'm on birth control," I gasp out, which doesn't sound great as a response to a conversation, but it's better than 'fuck just cum in me please'. My voice hitches on those words, and a burst of heat in my cunt, or maybe my clit, or just kind of that general area, I don't know anymore. I don't think I could tell my hands apart right now. I just know that the thought of him cumming in me is so completely appealing, it's enough to push me over the edge. My cunt spasms and clenches around his cock, eliciting a noise of need from him. A wave of pleasure so complete it knocks the breath out of my body moves through me.

Khent's own movements grow more harried and less elegant, rocking into me through my orgasm until he groans and stiffens. I feel the hot flood of his cum inside me, filling whatever space there's left.

He pulls out of me, the head of his cock glistening with a mixture of my wetness and his own cum.

I lay still on the ground but my legs are shaking, and with every residual pulse of my orgasm more of his spunk drips out of me.

He curls an arm around me, enveloping me in his embrace. We lay there on the floor, no words, just our breathing and heartbeats falling into step.

For the first time in weeks, the Blood Fever has almost entirely subsided. I can't remember when I last felt this relaxed, this comfortable and safe. Even before I broke his nose. I don't need to hold any kind of guard up because he's here, holding me.

Maybe I could try to believe in soul mates, for Khent's sake.

10

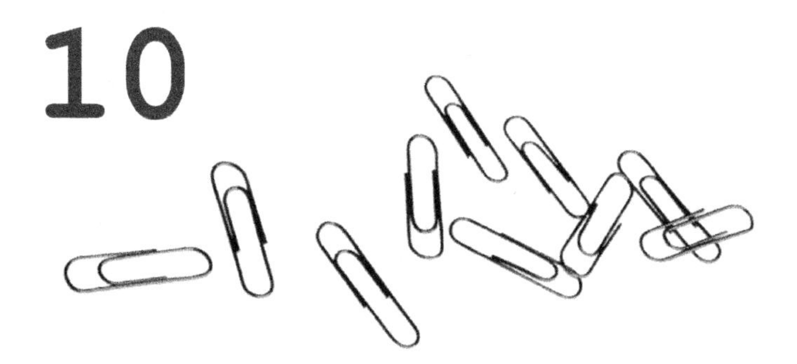

The key to making relationships work is setting healthy boundaries. Or, so I've heard. And that's the advice I give to friends because it sounds like a smart plan. Just because I'm mate-bonded with Khent doesn't mean I'm getting unhealthily attached. I'm just dating him the way I would date anyone.

Which starts with stealing one of his shirts.

Not really stealing, just borrowing it.

There isn't a lot of mattress space left in my bed when he stays over, so I roll off the top of him and land a little too hard on the floor.

I grab his button-down shirt off the floor and pull it on like it's a bathrobe, rolling the sleeves up a number of times before I head to the kitchen to make my usual eggs and toast.

“One or two eggs?”

“I don’t really eat breakfast,” he shrugs. He leans against my cabinetry as he threads his belt through his.

“You’ve said, and I cannot believe that,” I tell him. I can’t imagine not eating even a little in the morning. Usually, my stomach is what compels me to get out of bed. Two eggs barely sustain me till lunch, and eyeing Khent I can’t believe he doesn’t have at least a dozen.

“It’s my deepest flaw,” he shrugs, rolling his eyes with a smile.

I turned the stove off and slid the eggs onto their awaiting toast. I turned away from them to give Khent a good morning kiss, but of course it becomes anything but brief.

He takes a knee to come down to my height, shuffling his shirt off of me, putting his arms through the sleeves even as my hands thread into his hair.

When he’s halfway through putting his shirt on, he curls an arm around me, pulling me in and letting out this big sigh like he’s the most content person alive.

When he’s got me gathered up in his arms like this, I wish he would never let go. That the world could fall away and it would be just this until my stomach completely rebels.

But then my ‘You should be leaving now’ alarm starts to beep, making us shuffle away from each other. Overlord, I’m not even dressed yet.

“Should we both be late?” he hums, taking in my now borrowed-shirt-less body. One of these days, I’m going to convince him to leave without it.

“That’s a dangerous question,” I return, shivering as his gaze sweeps down my skin.

“We could be very, very late.”

I tilt my neck back and feel the way his tusks graze my skin as he trails kisses down my neck and collar. My hands trace down his shoulders… and start buttoning up his shirt.

We’ve already been very, very, very late twice.

“You go, I’ll catch up,” I tell him. “Probably in the parking lot because you’ll have passed out from not having breakfast.”

“Hasn’t happened yet.”

“One day,” I tug on his tie and he leans in for another kiss goodbye. He doesn’t even fully kiss me back, he’s smiling too hard, the nerd.

Then he’s out to go pick up a change of clothes from his place before work, and I’m standing naked in my kitchen, waffling back and forth between getting ready and kind of staring at the door after him.

I do mean it. I can see a day when our routines will have finally meshed together seamlessly. And I will finally make him see how vital a meal breakfast is.

This has been our routine for the last week or so. Somehow, I still get to work mostly on time, and Bill has observed my abnormally chipper mood of late.

"I don't want to get into trouble with HR," I text Khent during a particularly boring meeting, my phone hidden behind a stack of binders I have on the table. "Or Monsters Resources."

Employee relationships aren't exactly forbidden, but considering the bureaucratic hoops you have to jump through so the company can guard itself against sexual harassment lawsuits, personal injury suits, property damage filings, and other things, they might as well be.

I've led enough employees through exactly that kind of paperwork. I've done the explaining what it all means and the legal clauses and how all this is important to maintaining a professional evil work environment.

I've seen employees go from puppy love to falling out of love after filling out everything in triplicate. It'd honestly be easier just to make pre-nups for everyone involved.

"Think about the paperwork we'd have to do for MR and HR," I type, not really giving him a chance to respond to my first text. "Especially after all the paperwork following up the filing cabinet incident."

Especially considering we were instructed to avoid each other to avoid liability issues.

After a few minutes of me constantly unlocking my phone to see if he responded yet, he sends back, "We'll be fine."

He adds a smiley with a capital C instead of a singular parentheses. *C:*

I like his nonconforming smiley faces. They seem bigger and goofier than the standard parenthesis conveys.

"Still, maybe we can keep things on the down-low at least."

A little bit later, he sends me a lowercase face. *c:*

I bite back against my own grin. Who knew there was this adorkable Orc hiding in the IT department all these years?

All around the meeting table, my coworkers look like they're either falling asleep with their eyes trained on the powerpoint presentation, or like they've gone to some deep recess of their soul. No wonder nothing gets accomplished in meetings and we end up repeating everything again in follow up emails.

I school my face into something similarly bored. I wouldn't want them to wonder what's up with me by looking excited to get to work.

It was a feeling that was increasingly hard to keep under wraps. My mind would wander into coming up with excuses to interact with Khent at work. The next few days were a blur between the heightened moments of passing notes to each other tucked into documents, pretending not to look at each other too much when we passed in the hallway, but still brushing shoulders. In stolen moments, we'd been exchanging flirty emails that are not nearly as covert as we thought we were, about floppy drives and uploading my data onto his hard drive.

I'm happier than I've been in a long time.

The next day, I stop in the office lobby, lingering by the front desk. I'm pretending I have a reason to fritter away moments because I don't want to go up to my desk just yet. I know I said I wanted to keep things hush at work, but I want one more glance at him before I start my day.

I catch Khent out of the corner of my eye and try not to look too excited at the prospect of running into him in the lobby. We see each other so sparingly in person during work, it gives me a little rush just to walk past him. Something about being around him makes the skirt I'm wearing feel so much shorter.

I swear I can feel the heat radiating off of him as he brushes past. I gripped the counter of the lobby desk as I scribble nonsense on a sign-in page that is really just for visitors. Goosebumps raise up on my skin and the familiar ache between my legs hits me so suddenly my knees shake. It's really for the better that we spend most of our work day several floors apart.

Since our relationship started and I've been seeing Khent after work and getting my back blown out nightly, the Blood Fever has all but died down. I barely notice it during the day, unless I run into him and it flares up again. I'd imagine that there's likely also something about being pumped full of Orc cum nightly that calms the raging fever down. But I'm no scientist.

Maybe it's because of that oil stuff I got from the holistic place. I set up a little mug warmer at my desk that I put a drop of it on every few hours. It's tempting to just dab a little on my wrists and rub them together like a perfume, and just smell that warmth incarnate on myself all day. The thing that stops me from doing that is the memory of buying that little bottle and the girl behind the counter telling me that a lot of people use it as lube. And after some additional research, apparently using it as lube during the mating ritual is pretty common.

But during a company-wide meeting all I could do was sit and thirst from across the room, gripping my chair and hoping I wasn't going to charge across the table to climb him like a tree. The thought had crossed my mind several times and almost seemed like a good idea many of them.

I hold still and scribble circles on the corner of the page like I'm trying to get ink out of the pen while Khent crosses to the elevators and presses the button. I breathe slowly and carefully listening as it arrives, the doors trundle open and he gets in, the carriage creaking under his weight.

I don't hear the doors close though, and turn around to look.

He's holding the elevator door open and as my eyes meet his, he raises his brows.

Sharing an elevator with Khent. Heat blooms across my skin at the thought and my body moves before my brain fully processes it.

The elevator door closes behind me and I'm hooking my fingers in Khent's belt loops, looking up at him. He glances away, holding back a smile.

Even with the elevator's mirrored walls, I can feel how little space there is in here. When I turn around to push the button for my floor, my ass brushes up against him. I stretch and do it again just so he knows it was entirely on purpose.

The elevator's machinery begins to whir, the floor jerks and I let myself use it to fall back against him. I tilt my head back against his sort of the lower end of his chest to glance up at him through my eyelashes. I can see the color in his cheeks just before he lifts a hand to trace my jawline. His other hand drags up my hip, palming the fabric of my skirt upwards. I grind back against him harder.

“I take it we need to go to your office and fill out some paperwork?” he murmurs, voice so low it goes straight to my clit.

“Fuck the paperwork,” I gasp, gathering up fistfuls of my pencil skirt, hiking it up enough to actually do more than tease. His hand curls fully around my thigh, giving me something to grind desperately against.

My heart is beating out of my chest when he leans forward to hit the emergency stop switch, bringing the elevator to a halt between floors.

The lurch sends me forward, I catch myself against the mirrored wall, the cool surface a stark contrast against my skin. Khent drags a thick finger through my cunt, until it’s slick enough to enter me.

I'm still a little sore from our antics last night at my apartment, but in some ways that heightens the sensation of it all. I move my hips experimentally as his finger slides in and out, the smallest of moans riding on my breath.

We don't have much time before someone notices the elevator isn't working, but the thought of being able to watch ourselves in the mirrored walls is making me wetter by the second.

I turn around, unbuttoning my blouse. His cock is straining against his pants, which I imagine must have some fantastic tensile strength to be able to contain him.

"I need you in me. Now. Right now," I breathe, a combination of words that's becoming a habit, almost a ritual between us.

The look he gives me is the same look he's given me the last few nights between my place and his. He raises an eyebrow, a smile tucked away behind a tusk. He thinks he's so fucking cute, I swear I'm going to bite him if he tries telling me to ask politely again.

He corrals me into his arms, holds my chin, kissing my forehead, my nose, and mouth in turn. He wants to see how long he can tease me before I'm practically begging for his cock. I make another noise of impatience, staring at him, starting to undo his belt and zipper my goddamn self.

He rolls his eyes and takes a knee in front of me. It does make it easier for me, even if I have to stand on my tiptoes to get things started.

He lifts and steadies me with a hand on my hip with a familiarity that almost makes me blush. I bite back any comment about being able to do this myself. I watch the reflection as he guides me down onto the head of his cock. My hands find fistfuls of his shirt as we start to move together, and I take more and more of him in me with each thrust. I'm not saying we should record porn of us, but I am surprised I've never seen human/Orc porn before.

He pushes my bra aside and dips his head to flick his tongue across one nipple, sucking and licking and kissing my tits, treating each of them in turn. As his tongue worked away at my breast, the pleasure he gave only increased the ache and need in my pussy. It snags my attention how he knows what I like, that a little more sensation while he's rutting into me is enough to push me over the edge.

Somewhere between the sensation of and the sight of him pounding into me, I break.

"Fuck, Khent, I'm–" I can't even manage a verb before I'm gasping for breath with a cry.

If there's one thing the Blood Fever has taught me, his orgasm will quickly follow mine. I can feel his release course into me, hot and wet. I can't think about how I'm going to figure out how to clean up after this, all I can do is ride the aftershocks of my orgasm and try not to rip the buttons off his shirt.

We slow our movements until it's just our breathing, holding each other loosely, our foreheads touching, the way he held me in his gaze and the way I couldn't even meet his eyes through my blush. It's just a touch too intimate, even after all we've done together. It's just something too much to know he's looking at me like I'm wonderful and I can see that soft smile on him. I can't put my finger on it, but it makes me want to take myself out of the equation. Like a sunlight so bright I need to shield my eyes from it. A warmth you could either melt or burn under.

I pull away first, running my hands through my hair and shaking off the afterglow.

My hair is a mess and my tits feel like they've been shuffled around in my bra.

I pull down my skirt from where it's hiked up around my hips, despite the cum I can feel starting to stick between my thighs. When we're sort of tidied up, he presses the button again, gets the elevator moving. A moment later the doors are opening on the IT department.

"Here's where I get off," he says, tucking his shirt in, cheeky smile and all.

I'm holding myself up against the elevator wall. I snort. "Yeah you do."

He blushes, running a hand through his tousled hair. "I didn't mean it like–"

"Yeah you did. See you later, nerd," I return, scrunching my nose at him.

He waves goodbye to me and that little gesture makes my knees weak. The doors rattle shut and I'm left alone, smiling like an idiot.

I never thought it was possible to be this happy.

The elevator begins to move upwards again, and I push off the wall. My legs are starting to regain some amount of steadiness, but I'm definitely going to collapse in my chair once I get into my office.

I turn to the mirrored walls, no longer fogged up by two of us panting in these tight quarters, and start to adjust my appearance, hopeless as that seems. Even if I don't run into anyone in the twenty feet from the elevator to my door, I still look like I've been jogging for an hour. Not to mention the cum still sticking between my thighs.

I'm fixing my hair when I spot it, and it makes my blood run cold.

The little red blink in a black lens tucked away in the ceiling corner.

It was never safe to be this happy.

11

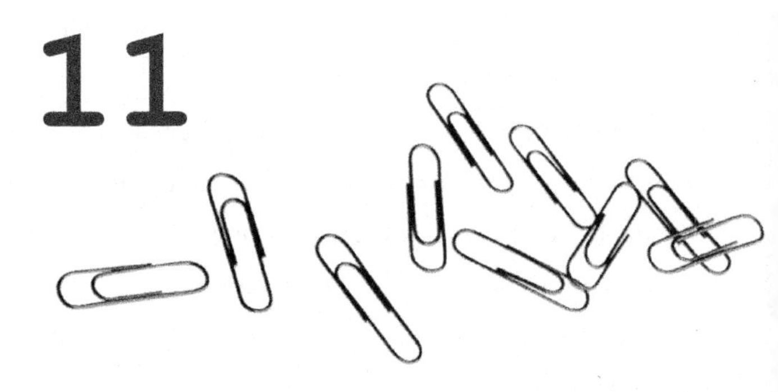

I return to my office and clean myself up as best I can.

For several minutes, it's all I can preoccupy myself with, because otherwise something in me is going to fracture. My heart's racing, but I feel like I can't think. I don't want to.

Maybe the cameras don't work, I try to reassure myself after a bit, mostly so I don't start hyperventilating as my brain desperately tries to switch into problem solving mode. Problem solving is what I do, everyone always turns to 'Janice from HR' to solve things.

But sitting alone in my office, the answer never comes.

"How are those personnel file updates going?" Melanie greets me at the door for our next meeting.

I stare back at her, unable to come up with any real answer. That's the last thing on my mind right now. When I realize I don't really have an answer for her, I make a noncommittal noise that leaves it open to interpretation.

"It looks like it," she returns, before she hits the lights and begins a slideshow.

The next hour and a half passes slowly, me nodding along whenever someone pauses, making thoughtful noises whenever someone asks a question. I don't contribute anything real and I don't think anyone notices.

Who really checks those cameras anyway?

I chew on my nails for a few minutes, not even partially convincing myself. I remember when some monitors suddenly went missing from the office a few months ago, they had checked the elevator tapes to find the culprit.

In some part of my gut, I knew this was coming. I've been so stupid, so reckless. I should never have given in to everything I was feeling with Khent. It wasn't ever going to be all flowers and sunshine, I shouldn't have wanted to think that it could have been.

Would sneaking back into the elevator and hitting the camera with my stapler make it all go away?

I marinate on the thought for several minutes, and as cathartic as it seems like it would be, that wouldn't work. They probably store the footage in one of the security offices.

I think on it for a while, each crossed off half-baked idea sinking me further and further into depression.

"...And from the elevator–"

"What?" I snap, and my head turns to look at my coworkers so fast my glasses slide down my nose.

They kind of stare back at me, surprise across their faces.

"I said the email from the systems administrator," Bill repeats for me, a creak of concern in his ancient voice.

"Oh," I say weakly, realizing I misheard.

My coworkers exchange glances and internally shrug it off. Conversation takes a moment before it picks back up to a normal pace. I just try to survive the meeting without looking like I'm trying to hide behind a notebook.

When it ends and I get to hide in the quiet of my office again, collapsing into my chair with a swiftness that makes my glasses clatter onto my desk.

I sigh and grind the heel of my palms into my eyes, smearing my makeup no doubt.

There's nothing I can do.

Someone was going to see that footage. Someone was going to see me and Khent making wildly inappropriate usage of company property. Someone was going to file a report about it, and then the pair of us were going to be sent to MR.

Maybe it wouldn't be today. Maybe it wouldn't happen tomorrow, or even this week. But sooner or later, someone was going to check that footage.

Was it worth it? To be constantly looking over my shoulder? For when this relationship would trip me up and be my professional downfall? Whether it was the elevator security footage or something else, it was going to happen. I've been here before, I know how it goes.

I'm replaceable, all employees are.

Being in HR, you get to know that better than anyone. No quicker way to sweep up liability issues than to let a worker go over the first blip.

And I'm going to take the fall, again.

I closed my eyes and massaged my temples, pushing my fingers up into the mess of my hair. Human resources didn't help me then, I doubt Monster Resources will help me now.

I just wasn't going to wait around to get fired.

My laptop pings. Just yesterday the message notification noise that had made my heart flutter wildly, feels like a little crack in my chest now.

I turn to my computer somehow both listless and panicked.

I fidget for several minutes and agonize over the keys and eventually send a single line email: There was a camera in the elevator.

My focus is scattered as I slowly wade through paperwork, not letting myself obsessively refresh my inbox the way I want to. I need to hear from him even if it hurts.

I break after 10 minutes.

Khent's reply is there, easygoing as he is, like he doesn't understand what it means. "If you're worried about it, I can pay the security room a visit. I'm sure their system is overdue for a check."

It tears a new crack in my heart to read, to want to follow that flutter of hope and trust him that it's that simple, it's that easy.

But if not the elevator, it was going to be somewhere else. A janitorial closet, the parking lot, in my office again when someone came by to drop off a report. As long as we were together, we were going to find other ways to deflower office property. One day we were going to slip up in a way we couldn't come back from, and it was going to be just like it was with James, all over again.

I thought I knew what heartbreak felt like but this is finding new pieces of me I didn't know existed. They're unguarded and tender to pain. I chew my lower lip and peck at the keys, carving out a response.

"It's not just about the camera. That can't happen again."

Each short response is all I can tear out even though it's not enough to finish the job.

I weigh the familiar feeling of heartbreak against the lesser-known feeling of breaking someone's heart. I don't think I've really had to do that before.

I hate myself for letting it get this far. Not just for my own feelings, but for how I've gotten tangled up in Khent's life. I feel like I've led him on by letting myself give in to the fever. If I had just stayed away from him, he never would have had his heart trifled with, he might have found a mating bond with someone else, someone more deserving of him.

He might have never even believed we were going to be something special because of this bond.

I've never had it in me to believe something as earnest and vulnerable as that. This was the direction it was heading all along, after all. It was never going to work out.

I look around my office, eyes sweeping from the test from the phishing training, to the spa receipt stubs, and the little bottle of oil I'd brought home from that day.

Everything I'm going to put in a box to forget about, after.

There's another ping, another message from Khent. I can almost hear the way he would say it, the quiet surprise in his voice. "No more sharing elevators?"

What I'm about to do is cowardly. I've given a lot more respectful goodbyes to guys a lot less good to me than Khent was. Usually I make a point to do this in person, but I can't see that happening in our particular circumstances. I've never broken up with someone over text or phone before, and certainly never email.

But it was going to hurt no matter what. I could either save myself all the time and feelings that were ever going to happen between me and Khent and end things now, or wait for it to hurt more later.

"No more anything."

He doesn't respond after that.

I had hoped before when we first got entangled in all this, that I was replaceable, for Khent's sake. Now I hope the same thing, but it nearly breaks me in half to try.

12

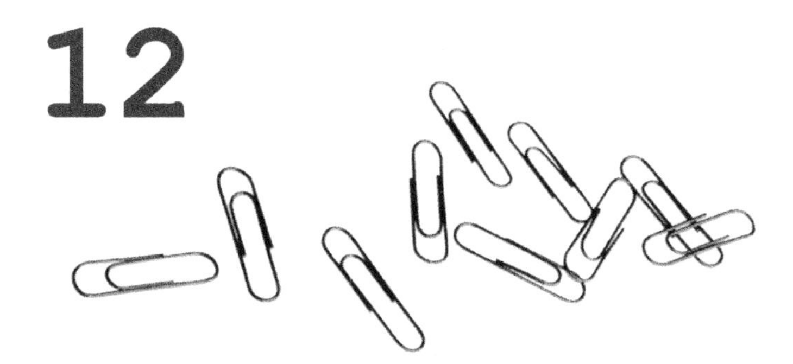

"Here are the personnel reports, Bill," I sigh, depositing a stack of folders on his desk.

He raises an eyebrow at me, wrinkling his papery skin. "Already?"

I've been focusing on work lately, like I should have been all along. I might be scaring my boss with a new level of productivity and engagement in meetings.

Anything to not think about it.

"Let me know if you need any more changes made," I tell Bill, and leave before he can say anything else.

To my relief, the constant ache of want and need that used to live between my thighs is gone. Or at least, it's migrated.

Most of the time now it sits on my clavicle, and every time I sigh it hollows out my chest a little more.

It was the right decision, I tell myself for the hundredth time.

I tell myself that a few more times as an email from Monster Resources shows up in my inbox, sending a spike of panic into my chest.

Reading the email does little to stem the anxiety brewing in my chest. Gwen from that first MR meeting is requesting a follow up, suggesting a few hours from now if my calendar is open.

That's really just a formality, the company has calendar sharing software. She's probably already checked my calendar and knows I'm free.

There's always an impending sense of doom when working at Evil Co, but it's been heavier lately. I've been wondering how long it would take someone to find that elevator security footage and report it. The worry had haunted my every moment.

And now that wait is over.

It tears little rips in my chest to ping Bill and Melanie that I'm going to miss our usual coffee break chat.

Melanie writes back a quick, "But I brought hazelnut coffee creamer this week!" to which Bill types out an emoticon I cannot discern the expression of.

I don't tell them that I'm probably not going to any other informal coffee breaks.

In some way, that email from MR both heightens my anxiety and relieves it: I know where this is going, I've been here before.

But the difference is this time, I know how to survive it.

I've been updating my resume and cover letter bit by bit the last week or so, deleting a word, rewriting it, then replacing it again with a word that's probably just as good. I've been checking job listings and filling out my information over and over again, a process that is as inefficient as it is torturous, the crown jewel of evil empirism.

I've done everything to protect myself right. I'll come out of this better than I did the last time.

It doesn't feel like it, though. It still hurts in all the places I thought I was putting armor over.

I send back a short reply to Gwen, and start going through my desk. I start tossing things in the trash, making a pile of things I can take home. I log out of all my accounts, halfheartedly thinking it'll make things easier for whoever has to reset the machine and make a login for the next employee.

I pack my purse with as much as will fit in it, and stack everything else on one end of my desk. Maybe I'll get a cardboard box from Gwen and I don't need to make multiple trips to get everything back to my car. Something about having to make more than one trip feels like it would sap my dignity.

I watch the clock tick down to my meeting with Gwen.

I should take the elevator. I don't like going into the elevator anymore because it makes me think too much about that moment, that free, wild with abandon, recklessly happy moment. When I take the elevator now, I feel the electric stare boring into me.

But Khent's more likely to take the stairs. He doesn't like how the swiftness of the elevator makes his ears pop.

I sigh and try not to dwell on the memory of when he had told me that, one of the nights at his apartment when I'd wondered aloud how we had never run into each other before. Just another thing I need to crumple up and put in the wastebasket.

Such a small detail, so inconsequential. And dumb, too. Who cares that he has a sensitive inner ear? It shouldn't feel like a treasure.

So I should take the elevator, to avoid him.

A few minutes before the appointmented meeting time arrives as I'm scrolling absently through my phone. I sigh and it takes a few tries to find the strength to push away from my desk, gather myself up for the meeting. I straighten up my appearance before heading out into the hall.

It's quiet in the halls. In a way, corporate buildings all look alike on the inside. There's not going to be much I miss about the place. Maybe a couple people I was close with, like Lily. Maybe we'll friend each other on ChainLinkedin. And finding somewhere else to work means I'll leave all the mess of these last few weeks with Khent behind.

I round the corner, and might as well have walked into a wall.

I know it's him before I even open my eyes.

I look up and he's got a monitor under one arm and probably a mile of DisplayPort cables bundled under the other.

Suddenly this building with dozens of floors is just too small, and we keep ending up in the same hallway, awkwardly trying to shuffle around each other. It hasn't gotten any easier.

We don't say anything, we don't look at each other. We move past each other quickly, but also not so quickly like we're trying to act like we're avoiding each other.

I don't know who the charade is for, each other or ourselves.

Gwen is waiting for me in the same empty conference room as before, etching something in the tiniest handwriting ever in her notebook.

She gives me the same polite yet unnerving smile she did when I first met her a month ago. I don't know what it is but

I'm convinced she must not be human, even if she appears to be.

"Good to see you, how have you been?" She asks as I sit down, and the question stops me.

Is she asking to be polite, as a greeting, or in reference to the Blood Fever Fiasco?

It's incredibly tempting to just lie and say everything is going well, to whichever one she means. But if she's seen the elevator tapes she knows Khent and I haven't been avoiding each other the way we said we would. She knows how irresponsible we've been.

"Eh," I say, as noncommittal as a syllable gets, after too many beats have passed. I pair it with a shrug. "Work, y'know."

She gives me a light, undeserved chuckle, brushing past my terrible conversation to the point of this meeting. She flips a manila folder open. The document text on the inside is also smaller than I can read from across the table.

She interweaves her fingers, propping her elbows up on the table, and lays her chin across her knuckles. I half expect her to reveal fangs as she levels her stare at me.

I brace myself. She doesn't need fangs to terrify me, just the words "security footage".

"So… out of the woods?" Gwen asks, eyeing me.

I blink. It takes a moment before I realize that she asked me a question. Wouldn't she be the one to tell me that?

"Sorry?"

"Well normally it's supposed to clear up pretty quickly after a bond is solidified, but the process of resisting it tends to draw things out," she says, like she's informing me of the weather, glancing down to her documents. "And there's no real data on what to expect for how long it affects humans."

My mind takes longer than it should to realize she's talking about the Blood Fever, and somehow we're not in the middle of firing me.

"So it's really up to you to tell us where you're at in this process."

"Tell you if I'm still experiencing the Blood Fever," I clarify, a little more bluntly than I should.

"Yes. And we had discussed it, rewrote some policies during the last month, since we didn't really have anything in place for this kind of circumstance. If you feel you still need it, you're free to take an extra week of sick leave."

"Even though it lasted more than a week?"

The question falls out of my mouth because it would if this were a policy I was helping to write.

Gwen gives a little shrug, making a face briefly as if to say she knows it's not fair, but that's corporate for you. "You're able to still take that week if you feel you need it."

Weirdly generous for Evil Inc., but then again that's the card to play to avoid legal action.

I contemplate it. I don't think I'm in a place where taking time off would be healthy. I'd wallow in my pajamas and rewatch twenty seasons of HGTV shows and order takeout for every meal and not shower once the whole time. At least going to work moves me through the motions of resembling a functional human being.

I shake my head.

"I just have a little survey for you to fill out," Gwen says, and pushes a form across the table.

It's a bunch of questions and check-yes-or-no boxes, and a line for me to sign my name at the bottom. It's a form to tie up all the ends and assure the company I'm not going to sue them over the incident. That they can just file the last month of my life away in a box to be forgotten in some storage closet, because everything is fine now.

Everything is fine? I mean, I guess she's not firing me, and I'm no more mated to a coworker than I was before all of this started. I guess by those standards, everything is fine.

Except that it still feels like my heart has sunk down into my stomach to live there, and sinks a little more every time I think about Khent.

I get a little more numb with every box I cross off, no I did not sustain injuries due to the incident, and no I was not bonded to a coworker. I scribble my name on it and push it back towards her.

She initials the paperwork and starts packing it into that manila folder. I half want to ask her if the elevator cameras still work, just to make sure.

"What would have happened if it… if we…"

I can't find the words to finish my question.

Gwen pauses in her paper shuffle. She tilts her head to the side to consider it. "If it wasn't over yet? You'd have that extra sick leave."

I shake my head. "No, I mean, if we had gone through with the bond."

"There… would have been more paperwork. To ensure there wasn't harassment or coercion on either side. Then some legal proceedings to make sure the company wouldn't play any role should the bond be annulled later on. Possibly some rearranging in departments to make sure no one involved in the bond was a direct report…"

I stop listening as she continues on, illustrating the sticky situation it could have been.

"Gotcha," I nod, standing up quickly.

Gwen stops listing various types of paperwork and stares at me.

"If that's all…?" I start to say, fumbling for an excuse.

"That's all," she nods, and I hurry from the room.

I was so sure I was going to be fired. Had I just built all that up in my head?

I'm sitting back at my desk a half hour later, realizing I shouldn't have logged out of everything. Not being fired, I kind of needed access again.

Had I freaked out over nothing?

No, the footage existed. It was there and it was a ticking time bomb. I wasn't crazy to think that I could get in real trouble over that. We could still get in real trouble.

But maybe I had overreacted. Maybe I had gotten so wrapped up in the idea that the exact same thing that had happened to me before would happen, all over again, that I hadn't been able to see things for what they were.

Khent wasn't like James. James had lashed out over a bruised ego. Khent had done nothing but exude warmth and caring…and fucking responsibility! This whole time he had held himself accountable for every little thing, even stuff he didn't need to, because he'd been so focused on my comfort level.

Shame bloomed up and down my neck, hunching my shoulders as I curled in on myself.

I wish I'd done that all differently. I wish I'd put his considerations on par with my own. I wish I hadn't been so quick to protect myself that I was willing to hurt him over it.

The whole mate-bonding incident shoved us together when we wouldn't have otherwise looked twice at one another, but I did like him. Even after the Blood Fever was over, I really liked him. I missed him and his dumb jokes and his lowercase smiley faces.

But… the Blood Fever was over. We weren't bound to each other in the way we had been before, there wasn't any reason to reach out to him, to talk to him. We had our separate lives on separate floors.

There wasn't any reason he would want to be around me anymore. Especially not with how I had ended things.

13

Getting back into my work laptop and the various accounts it connected to is a long process that only further illustrates why the IT guys hold onto a laptop for a week before they give it to new hires. There's too much to set up.

Yesterday after my meeting with Gwen had been close enough to 5pm that I just went home instead of dealing with it, leaving it for the morning.

Returning the next morning with fresh eyes did not make the process any easier.

It's a lot of entering the same password and email address into different accounts and applications. I know there's probably some IT protocol that I should have followed to make all the passwords unique, but I can't really bring myself to give a damn when this way just makes it easier.

I message one of my coworkers for the shared accounts' info, the logins that use the generic hr@evil.co address that everyone in the department can access.

It doesn't take all morning, just an hour or so. The tediousness of the task makes that hour feel like several.

Then I hit a wall.

None of the email addresses work on one of the portals, the one for approving PTO requests. I enter the department email again and again, and after I put the password in, it takes me to a page saying the account doesn't exist. None of my coworkers remember what the account information is because none of them ever bother to log out of it.

I stare at my screen a while longer, fingers resting tensely on the keys, willing myself to remember something that is just not there.

After I try the same email addresses a couple more times, hoping it was a small typing error that threw the process off, and all of my attempts getting the same screen of failure, I slouch down in my chair in frustration.

I can't do this on my own.

I dial the IT Department general number and try not to cringe at myself for knowing it by heart. I have to hang up and do it again when I nearly dial Khent's extension number.

It rings a few times, and I chew my lip hoping I don't get Khent. Hoping anyone else will pick up.

Am I really calling the IT Department over something so small?

I'm in the middle of contemplating hanging up when a familiar voice answers, and my heart sinks into my stomach.

"IT Department, how can I help you?" Khent says, his voice friendly as usual, though a little tired.

He doesn't sound particularly upbeat, not that I would have expected him to. Hearing him happy right now might bury me alive.

I'm quiet for way too long trying to pull some other insight from the tone of those few words.

"Hello?" He repeats.

"Hi! Uh, yeah. Um," I fumble with the phone.

"Oh," Khent says, a note of surprise and not much else I can decipher when he recognizes my voice.

"Yeah," I sigh, sinking further into my chair, kind of acknowledging that I don't want to be calling him either. If only crawling under my desk would allow me to escape this moment. Maybe the floor could conveniently swallow me up like it does when the boss gets in a mood.

"Um, I, uh, accidentally locked myself out of the admin side of the PTO Request portal. It keeps saying my account doesn't exist, but I don't think I deleted it."

I twist the desk phone's curly cord between my fingers anxiously in the silence.

"Can you tell me what email address I'm supposed to use to log in?" I ask after too many beats and too many breaths have passed and I'm starting to wonder if he's not going to answer me because I don't deserve it.

"Evil Co One," he says. I can't get anything from his voice.

A few seconds of silence stretch by, waiting for him to add the @ and a dot com in there. It never comes.

I clear my throat and try again, "Which one?"

"The Evil Co. address," he states again, and I can't help but notice it's still not an email address. I don't know what was wrong with my question.

I humor him and type 'Evil Co. One' into the address bar, and surprise, it doesn't work because that's not an email address.

"I don't know what that address is," I say after grumbling through mashing the backspace bar.

"…It's your email address. Just use your own work email."

My cheeks burn. I don't think I've ever felt dumber. Why hadn't I tried that?

The words start piling up in my chest, apologies that don't feel good enough to say, winding up and tightening my throat.

I want to tell him I had been spinning myself into some kind of anxiety attack that day, that I wished I hadn't hurt him, that he hadn't deserved to be pushed away with an email.

I should have at least given him the chance to hear his response in person, to perhaps refute the knee jerk reaction I was having.

But it's too much to wonder how that could have gone differently, to wonder if I still had a chance of patching that up. I couldn't ask that of him when I had already done so much damage.

Khent speaks before I can get any words out.

"You don't have to worry about the elevator footage. I put a magnet on top of the security tape shelf."

My throat is too tight for the small laugh to get through. My heart aches to tell him that's rather old school.

"I didn't ask you to do that," I say, and it comes out weaker than I want it to.

"You didn't have to," he answers simply, a deeper note of emotion coloring his words. It's open and caring the way he's always been, in the way I should have known he was.

I press the phone hard against my face because my hand starts to tremble. I bite my lip closed so it doesn't wobble.

"I'm sorry–" I start to say, when dial tone starts buzzing in my ear. I don't know if he heard me.

I dig through the box of things I'd packed up and hadn't gotten through unpacking again, looking for the little mug warmer and the vial of claiming ritual oil. I set it up and as soon as I can feel any kind of heat coming off the mug-warmer, I tip a droplet onto it.

Not because I need it as some kind of anti-horny essential oil diffuser, but because I miss the warmth that smelling it made me feel. The sunlight-kissed coziness that was the same as seeing Khent smile.

But now, it doesn't smell like anything at all.

I blink, and after a few moments, sniff a few other things in my office to make sure my nose is still working. Stale vinegar chips and an air freshener tag confirm that it is.

I fall back in my chair, slumping a little more than before. Did the oil only smell like that because I'd been under the Blood Fever's spell?

Pretty much all of the Blood Fever symptoms were cleared up, and here I was, still missing him. I buried my face in my hands.

If I'd met him normally, got to know him normally, no nose-breaking fever-inciting accidents involved, I still would have really liked him. I'd have been charmed by his dorky little mannerisms and his unfunny jokes and probably still come to the conclusion that I wanted to ride his tusks in a non-supernaturally charged horniness kind of way. I don't give a damn about soulmates or whatever, he made my days better just by being there.

I had to stop stewing in my office at some point. The thing that ended up wrenching me out of my chair was that I had a meeting in fifteen minutes. I figured being surrounded by people and having to think about something that wasn't how much of an idiot I'd been lately would be better.

But my bad luck wasn’t done with me today.

Not halfway to the meeting, I spotted him down the hall, maybe fifty feet. I wondered momentarily how I had never noticed how often we walked the same spaces and had never spoken to each other.

But after that phone call, I didn't think I could withstand another awkward encounter, even if it was as small as walking past him, pretending I wasn't making eye contact with him for a better reason.

I was just thinking that there was an empty conference room behind me that I could duck into and hide in while he walked down the hallway, when the fire alarm went off.

For the next moment, I had about one thought per second.

First, realizing it was just a fire alarm. The loudness of it had startled a little adrenaline into my system, but the familiarity of its blaring kicked in quickly.

Thud.

Second, that I could smell just a touch of burned popcorn. Jeez, who makes popcorn in the office? That and microwaving fish should just be banned.

Thud.

Third, I should turn around and head down a different staircase to the parking lot than Khent.

Thud.

Fourth, what was that noise?

Whatever I was going to think next was thrown aside as I was lifted up bodily. It didn't register so much as being picked up in my brain as it felt more like being knocked into, colliding with someone hurrying past.

Then there's the sounds of traffic and the outdoors, and I realize I'm draped over Khent's shoulder like a scarf, and he's currently scaling down the side of the office building.

Building. Outside. Ground.

The realization of what hanging off the side of the building really means comes staggered, slowly all together falling into place.

I'm torn between squeezing my eyes shut so I can't see how far off the ground we still are, and watching each grab at the side of the building he takes just to assure myself that we're not about to fall. Every movement he makes, digging his fingers into the brickwork, strong and even somewhat graceful, is still terrifying. I need a seat belt or a Janice bjorn or something, anything that's going to assure me he won't just drop me five stories. I nearly elbow him in the face trying to get my arms around his neck.

"Did you attend the same MR meeting as I did?" I squeak, because that's where my brain goes when nothing else makes sense. It's easier to focus on the fact we're supposed to be keeping our distance and this is the opposite of that, than it is to confront that we're dangling off the side of the building.

He stills, and after a moment I can bear to take a peek at him.

Khent has the audacity to look a little surprised himself. "Fuck."

"Fuck is not gonna cut it," I continue to shrill with no semblance of authority.

"I just– I heard the alarm and I didn't think. I just had to get my mate out– I mean," he tries to backtrack, but it's too late.

My mate. The words send warmth all through my core and relax all the muscles in my back. To him, we're bonded, not in the middle of a breakup. The part of me that was apparently still dealing with the lingering effects of the Blood Fever– ok, the part of me that actually really missed him, is cheerleading like I scored a touchdown.

"Sorry, I didn't mean to say that–" he starts to say.

"It's fine," I cut him off, even if that's not really the word for this. "I mean, we'll get to that later. Let's just figure our way out of this."

It's not sweet, it shouldn't be sweet. He can't be thinking of me like that. Why would he, after my shitty breakup email?

My mind has at least two teaspoons worth of rationality left, and it's enough for me to try to school my emotions, despite whatever my body is feeling. I take a moment to breathe and try to think through this.

The parking lot is on the other side of the building, and that's where everyone will be gathering to go through the fire drill procedures while we wait for the firetruck. Below us is just the empty alleyway between the two office buildings. We're maybe four stories off the ground. Still too high for my tastes.

In some attempt to not just be dangling in the wind, I try to wrap my legs around his incredibly broad waist. Even without being under the effects of the Fever, the movement is so familiar between us, it feels like home. Every part of my body that hadn't been involved in panicking aches to remember that comfort, that tenderness.

And between us, his cock is trapped between my body and his.

"You need to stop sliding around," he says, his voice low and a little wrecked.

My legs are only barely hooked around his middle as I've been trying to secure my safety. I may have not realized I was rubbing my body against his arousal.

I do not want to go back to Monsters Resources to explain this. Trying to do paperwork for this would just be mortifying.

The erection he's sporting against me is enormous. My body responds to his, and, my heart is between my legs, heat spreading in my lower belly as the need to be taken right here against the brick, stories off the ground, unfurls within me. The fleeting wonder if anyone across the way in the other office building will see us makes my nipples tighten.

Oh Evil Overlord, I'm so far gone.

It's actually insane how this wave of hormones completely wipes away my survival instinct. Getting dicked down on the side of the building? How do female Orcs survive this process? Scratch that, how does anyone?

"The ground. I'd like to be standing on solid ground," I manage after a moment. "I have to be present for my floor's roll call."

Khent nods. I brace myself for more of that stomach turning movement as he reaches to climb down, and bury my face in his shoulder. One breath is enough to make me forget the peril of our current position. I don't know how to describe scents like some kind of smell-sommelier, but it's all I ever want to breathe in ever again. This is what all men's scented deodorants should aspire to.

Holding him makes all the stress of the past weeks melt away. How could I have ever thought he'd be willing to hurt me the way James did?

Khent takes one step, or reach or whatever, and stiffens, and I think I know why. Now that I'm aware of how my cunt is all but pressed to the outline of his cock, every little shift in movement grinds our NSFW bits together.

If I could spare a hand from being clutched around his neck, I might just try to unzip him here. The sex against a brick wall might be worth the bruises and scrapes alone.

I realize then that I can't blame the Blood Fever's for the unhinged idea, it's just me, Unhinged Janice, with her fucking off the wall wants.

"I'm sorry–" he starts to say.

"No, it's ok," I try to cut him off.

"No, it's not. You don't want this," he says.

The friction is sweet and teasing, and agonizing in how much more I want. But I know he means I don't want this entanglement between us, this messy, against-company-policy relationship.

His jaw tightens and works as he holds still and climbs down a little more, to stop again. His head tilts back and I can see him fighting the pleasure.

His brow furrows and he shakes his head at himself, before pressing on.

"I feel terrible that I want you so much, but you don't seem to want that and I'm pressuring you and spilling my feelings and you don't need this crap right now."

He looks away from me, but I still catch the angst in his face. It's a reflection of what I've been essentially broadcasting since that first MR meeting, and every word of it he returns to me is a needle through my heart.

"But I want it anyway."

I feel his entire being still at that. He doesn't look back at me though.

The need to tell him everything starts welling up in my chest, my throat. Admitting that was like turning on the faucet to everything in me I was brushing off and shoving aside.

"I'm sorry I freaked out and hurt you. I got scared everything was going to blow up in my face and this time it was really going to hurt because I think I've fallen in love with you," I babble out. "And I thought it would be safer if I ended things. But I was wrong. Not being with you was so much worse."

I almost cringe at saying I've fallen in love, but he just called me his mate so I don't think it's too weird to be bringing that word into this now.

"I need to stop stepping on your feelings to preserve my own. Because that doesn't get us anywhere. I don't want to hurt you, ever again."

I wouldn't blame him if he didn't believe me. I've been so back and forth, so wishy-washy over this whole mating thing. I can't expect him to be all-in again after how I've behaved.

I feel him shift a little, and then he's freed one hand to tentatively curl around my back, holding me to him.

"Where does that leave us?"

"Well, if you'll let me," I say, and take a deep breath before I meet his eyes. "I'm going to break your nose again."

14

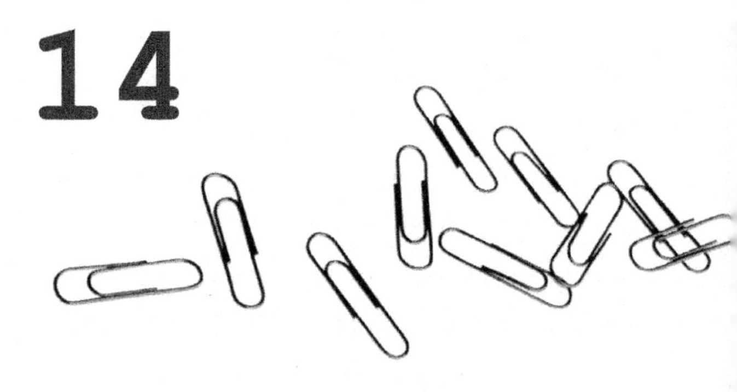

Khent raises an eyebrow. "Actually?"

He looks a little concerned, probably because he's not following my thought process.

"Um, I mean, only if totally necessary. I mean," I fumble with my words because that definitely sounded more like a threat and less what I really meant.

I try to reach my pockets, but my hands are a little preoccupied, keeping me from falling off the Orc holding us to the side of the building and all. "Can you…?"

He takes my meaning and nods. He cups a hand under my ass to support my weight as he shifts us down to some kind of ledge. The window that the architecture frames is covered up by curtains on the inside. It's not quite a balcony, but it's somewhat less precarious.

"I don't think you can get the Blood Fever to restart on purpose–" he's starting to say, when I pull the vial of oil from my pocket.

His eyes widen and I know he knows what I mean now.

"I want to do the claiming ritual," I say, just in case. But also because saying things out loud is important, and I need to tell him how much he means to me so he knows without a doubt. "I want to do what we would have done if I'd understood what the Blood Fever meant from the beginning."

He looks bashful for a moment, and then like he's going to say something, and then he decides against it.

"If that's still possible, and if that's something you want," I add quickly, but my attempts to give him room to say no are cut short by him drawing me close.

Khent tries to kiss me but he's so happy that he's just smiling against my mouth, the dork. But I say nothing, I'm smiling too. Then I casually slip my hand down the front of his pants.

Khent bites down on his grin, trying to hide that he was enjoying every second of it.

"I don't think we're allowed to mate on the side of the building," he murmurs out of the corner of his mouth.

"Don't see you stopping me."

Unhinged Janice is now in charge. I'm letting her have free reign because Calm and Collected Janice has not had great success with decision making.

"I think I know roughly how this works, but maybe you should start it," I say, undoing the vial's cap.

Khent moves us, so that my back is pressed to the window and he knelt on the ledge before me, one hand still holding the brickwork, locking us in.

"There's not much method to it," he said, taking the vial from me. He tipped the vial into my palms, showing me how to let it flow out in rivets along my fingers. His hand joined mine, soon the both of us had the oil covering our hands, our palms entirely stained with the ink.

"Alright," he said, nodding his chin to me, ready with enough oil on the top of his fingers.

I leaned forward with closed eyes, holding in a breath. After a hesitant moment, I felt him sweep his fingertips across my eyelids, grazing my lashes gently as any brush. He drew a few careful lines on my face, and I was touched by his attentiveness.

Forgetting my hands were still drenched in the ink, I took hold of Khent's face and kissed him for being so thoughtful. I rose up on my knees, sinking into the kiss as he received me, merging into his lap. I drew my thumb along his jaw, stroking his cheek as I kissed him deeper, brushing my tongue against his teeth. Eventually we broke apart, and we were left breathing heavily, holding each other's stare.

"Oh, oops," I giggle when I realize there are now matching palm prints on the sides of his face.

"You can mark me how you like," he shrugs, and I nod, bumping my nose against his.

He grins at that. His fingers kiss along my eyes with gentle dots, and sweep delicately across my cheeks, and over the bridge of my nose. I expand on the design on one side of his face and draw a pair of lines across the other side, continuing down his neck. He shrugs out of his shirt as I continue my design on his shoulder and spread it across his chest.

I want to touch him whole-handedly, but I know that unless I keep to only using my fingertips, I wouldn't be able to take my time with this. And I want to savor every second of this, to feel what it really meant to be unabashedly open with my feelings for Khent.

He marks my upper lip carefully with the ink, with a touch so tender and careful to avoid any mistake. I dare not breathe and disturb what he was doing. Somehow, it's more intimate than a kiss.

He wet the tips of his fingers in the oil again, and I feel a heavy drop of ink slip down my chin. It travels down, drawing a warm line of its own on my throat, before it slips down the valley of my breasts.

Without thinking, I caught his finger in my mouth. I licked a trail down the length of it, and sucked the oil off his finger.

“It’s got a bitter taste,” I say, surprised. “But I like it.”

Khent raises an eyebrow, and I can tell he wants to make a dumb joke about that. I roll my eyes and advance before he can say anything.

I put a handprint on his ribcage as I push him onto his back, crawling forward to straddle his waist. Propping himself up on his elbows, he looks over to see me lean over his knees, dragging my teeth against his hip bones. Wetting two fingers in the ink, I draw a line from his chest along his stomach, my other hand unzipping his pants.

With the oil, I draw careful lines down from his navel to his hardened cock, and press a kiss to his stomach, making my way ever lower.

My blood is simmering with that sun-kissed warmth, singing, wanting, craving.

My fingers, small and delicate against the enormity of his cock, trace the shape, the pattern of the veins up to the head. My eyes flick up to his face as he stifles a noise under my touch. I nuzzle my lips against the soft skin and he groans at the stimulation, lifting his hips in reaction.

I giggle again and take his cockhead into my mouth, my tongue swirling around it. He lets out something of a strangled moan as my lips draw him further into my mouth.

He closes his eyes, turning his face up towards the open sky, letting the pleasure show plainly on his face, though I saw how the brickwork under his hands was starting to crack with the grip he held onto it. It must have been all he could do not to curl his fingers in my hair and fuck into my mouth.

I pulled my mouth off him with a wet pop.

"Say it again," I tell him, flicking my tongue across his cockhead, and say, if only to see my mere words unravel him, "Call me your mate."

I watch his hips jerk in reaction as I lick the pre-cum that is beading over his slit. I give another teasing stroke to his cock, sitting up, slipping my other hand down to stroke myself through my pants, the fabric already damp.

His chest heaves with breath before his eyes lock with mine, and he growls, "You're my mate."

A burst of warmth in my chest nearly knocks me over at that. I have to hold myself steady between his knees.

The thought that he had wanted this as badly as I do, that he had ached with as much need as I had, was almost too much to take in.

He cups a hand under my ass and draws me up to his level, my legs scrambling to find purchase. Gently, he brings his lips to mine, and caresses slowly but vigorously.

Clinging to his shoulders, my legs gripped around his hips, my roving hands threaten to tear his shirt off, and then mine. I wanted him to see what a mess he made me, how easily his touch made me rosy-cheeked and breathless, helpless with desire.

I grin through my kisses up at him, moving my knees apart as he pulls off my pants. His hands slide up my thighs, finding me wetter than ever.

My hands are tangling in the disaster of his thick hair, pulling him in and holding him shamelessly as he ducks down to nuzzle my thighs.

His broad shoulders graze the insides of my knees as he kneels between them, his head bent, lashes dark on his cheeks. He parts me with his tongue, my hips bucking at the sensation.

I draw in a short breath, my fingers tangling in his hair as he searches around with his tongue, finding my clit and swirling his tongue around it, his tusks bruising my inner thighs. He licks up and down my cunt, the heat of his mouth too much to bear as he alternates between tonguing my hole and sucking my clit.

"Right there, oh, do that," I moan, my hips bucking into his mouth. I'm lost in my pleasure, finding salvation riding on the breaths of his name. "Khent, Khent, I want you in me–" I gasp, spreading my legs as wide as I can.

Khent stops short, looking up. "Are you sure?"

I lean up on my elbows to look at him, and I see the unspoken part in his eyes. A moment of hesitation, in case I don't actually want this and I'm just taken in by the moment.

But I want him to know I'm all in. I'm with him and I want this. I want to be mated to him.

Holding his gaze, I wet my fingers with the oil, and draw them down my leg. I curl my fingers inside my cunt, the slick oil mixing in. I was ready.

I watch his pupils darken and his nostrils flare as he breathes in my arousal.

I lean back against the glass of the window, watching as he oils up his heavy cock with a few slow tugs. Then he slips a finger inside me, down to the knuckle. I whine for more with every thrust, even as he adds one lubed finger after another.

Finally, he eases himself into me, little by little, stretching my cunt ever wider until it's nearly too much.

"Fuck, Khent," I gasp, "How much more of you is there?"

"Um, about halfway," he mumbles after a moment. He pulled back an inch or so, and suddenly I was achingly empty.

"No," I moan, no care for how needy I sound, how desperate I am to be fully sated. "A little more, come on just a bit further."

I hook my legs around his waist, and sink ambitiously down to the base of his cock.

"Fuck," he chokes, falling onto his forearms over me, pinning us to the window frame. I manage a grin through my wincing.

"This is not a competition," he manages to say after a moment. He looks like he wants to say something else, but his response is to gently move into me again.

"Then you should fuck me better than I can myself," I tease, trying to lift my hips into his again, but he stops me with a hand, holding me completely against the glass.

His large hand is braced against my stomach, holding me safe as he ruts into me, a finger poised just right to rub against my clit with each thrust, teasing me. Each movement, each sensation, pushed my pleasure a little further. He takes his time, nipping at my neck, rubbing my clit even harder till I'm shaking, my thighs are soaked and I'm about to beg for him to fuck me hard enough to make me pass out.

"Make me yours," I moan, and those are the words that make him lose the last shred of gentleness he was holding onto. "Claim me, please."

Every thrust pounds into me, and soon it's enough to push me over the edge. My fingers grip his shoulders and my nails dig into his back. I come with a gasp, or maybe a cry– I can't tell how loud I'm being anymore. All I know is as my back arches up with the feeling, my cunt squeezing around his cock as his body tenses.

I can feel his cock twitch before he comes, my cunt still pulsing with the aftershocks of my own orgasm. I feel the hot, seeping wave of his cum as he groans again, each spurt of it slowing his thrusts.

Between the waves of little tingles that reaches even to my toes and the feeling of his cum dripping out of me, I think I must pass out in his arms. The next time I blink, he has me curled up against him, draped over his body like my bones turned to jelly.

"I think I missed my floor's roll call," I mumble into his skin. I lean back just enough to give my thighs a once-over. Definitely messier than usual. I don't know where I'm going to find enough paper towels to clean this up. "I don't think I can show up looking like this anyway."

I look at Khent, and he's just giving me this utter look of tender love. My own expression softens, and my knee jerk need to say something cheeky again rises up.

But I don't say anything. I push back on the need to shield my heart. I can be vulnerable with him.

I take his chin in my hand, giving him a quick kiss. I could taste myself on his tongue, that salty, bitter, almost imperceptibly sour touch. "I don't know what words to use to tell you I love you. I don't know anything I could say would actually do the emotion justice."

"Just to hear you love me at all is enough for me," he says, stroking my cheek. "My mate."

Mate. I could get used to that.

15

"What about this one?" I ask, stopping in the open doorway of my bedroom. I've lost count of how many times I've done this. The first time I attempted to strike a pose, this time I just lift and drop my arms like it'll show off the sweater any better. I'm running out of energy.

Khent glances up from the stove, the whisk in his hand scraping the bottom of the pot. "My answer hasn't changed."

I grumble, because it's not a helpful answer.

"Babe, you look fine in everything. You're stressing yourself out over nothing," Khent says from the kitchenette.

He's making some kind of lichen-based soup, which, while it smells good, tastes like absolutely nothing to me. Vaguely reminiscent of cardboard, perhaps. I hope there's some leftover bouillon cubes in the fridge so I can mix half of one into my bowl.

He's making soup, I suspect, because I'm starting to stress him out.

I return to digging through my closet, tossing one thing after another onto my bed like a big, uncomfortable nest of nerves. I've pretty much run out of outfits to try out, and I still can't decide what to wear.

"She's going to love you no matter what."

"I know," I repeat for the tenth time. I can't really explain that this is as much a balm for my anxiety as it is exacerbating it. I do this every time there's some big event I feel like I'll be judged just for existing at.

"Then what's the problem?"

I just kind of grumble and moan through a non-answer. I know it's not all that important and that as long as I'm not wearing a t-shirt with an obscure gnome metal band, Khent's mom isn't going to think much about what I'm wearing.

Still, I wish I had some kind of manual to study. Or a script. Something to fall back on when I talk myself into a corner.

"Meeting your parents went well," he points out, like he can reason with my thought process.

"I mean, that's different. I'm pretty sure they still think we're just dating," I tell him, trying to keep my voice even, but there's a hitch of guilt that gives me away. I wince as I drop some more shoes on the ground. "You remember how utterly weird I was about the whole mating bond thing at first. If I introduce it slowly to them, I think it'll go over better."

I hear the stove click down to its lowest setting, the creak of the floor under his weight as he goes to sit on my couch.

"How slowly?"

"Maybe we could tell them we're mated… in a year?"

Khent hums a noise that I've now come to understand as 'why do humans take so long to do anything'.

Some of the time I agree.

I pluck the last few things out of my closet and frown at them. I toss them onto the pile and shuffle back out of my room. I sigh heavily and cross the apartment to flop onto his lap.

Looking up at him, I trace the lines of his jaw with my fingertips. He's borrowed one of my scrunchies to put his hair in possibly one of the worst buns ever constructed, and the black t-shirt he's wearing fits his shoulders extra snug. I wonder if I'll ever get used to seeing him out of work clothes.

"We still have to do all that paperwork for MR now," I remind him. "Wouldn't want to break the news until it was at least official."

"The paperwork isn't going to take a whole year," he says.

"Mmm," I hum playfully, but also because he's still underestimating how slowly things get processed.

"Think of it this way: they'll already have liked you for a while, so they'll be excited to hear the news. Even if they don't totally get what it means. And we're not telling them about the Blood Fever part," I ramble on, even though I know he doesn't need any more convincing. We're definitely in agreement on that. "Whereas, when I meet your mom, I have one shot to make a good impression."

I don't think he's listening, though, the hundredth time I've said that just melds with all the previous times. Hell, I'm tired of hearing me say it. His gaze goes distant and his eyebrows narrow. For a moment I wonder if he's staring at the stove, trying to figure out if he turned it down enough or not.

"Should we… be doing… the human equivalent?" he asks slowly, like he's not sure he's expressing himself right.

The human equivalent, of what, a mating bond? I don't think there is one. But I watch the distant expression on his face, like he's realizing he's forgotten something important.

I stare at him a few moments blankly before I realize what he means. I bolt up in his lap and put my nose to his.

He stares back at me, and after a moment, takes off his glasses because I am fogging them up.

"What?"

"You fucked up, just now."

He lifts an eyebrow, rubbing the corner of his t-shirt on the lens. "Did I?"

A maniacal grin spreads across my face. I kiss his neck and repeat gleefully, "You. Fucked. Up."

"I don't do this to you when you don't know about Orcish things," he points out. He's right, but unlike him, I enjoy annoying the people I love.

"And I don't make you order your own needlessly complicated coffee when we go across the street," I counter.

"No one needs to be as extroverted as those baristas," he sighs.

"They're not gonna bite," I roll my eyes, and drag my teeth along his jawline for effect. And for me.

He shifts in his seat, moving me with him. He props his head up in his hand, elbow on his knee as he looks at me. "So what'd I do wrong?"

I wriggle my way into a more comfortable position, laying out across the couch, my head in his lap. I can barely contain how evil this makes me feel. I'm going to show him videos of flash mobs and over the top public proposals. "First, the asking the question part is like, half of the whole thing. It's a big deal. I'm not even supposed to know you're gonna ask me."

"Why's that?"

"Because you don't know if I'm going to say yes or no."

Khent scoffs, because that part is clearly ridiculous to him. "You're my mate. Why would you say no?"

"Secondly–"

"There's more?"

"SECONDLY," I push on, extra determined now, "Some people make as big a deal about it as the actual ceremony."

"Oh?"

"Yeah. They get fancy about it. Some people wait until they're in front of everybody they know, and then get everyone's attention on them. And then they ask the question, not knowing how it's going to turn out," I whisper, like I'm telling a campfire story.

I'm quick to pull my phone from my pocket, and start searching videos of public proposals gone wrong. I scroll for a moment, looking for a particularly awful one that Lily had sent me a while back.

I glance back at Khent when I can't find it, and realize he's gone stone-still, and deeply quiet.

"Babe?"

This big guy who can't make his way through a coffee order without apologizing four times, and won't make eye contact with strangers unless he absolutely has to, looks like he's actually considering everything I just teased him with.

It looks like it takes him every effort to ask, "And… that's something you want?"

The look on his face softens my heart and melts away the mischief that had possessed me a moment ago. I reach up and touch his face, brushing my thumb against his cheek.

"I've already got what I want."

Gwen

I swear to Evil Overlord, we just wrapped this up.

I'm staring across the table at one Orc, and one human, whose combined Monster Resource file is now a couple inches thick.

Smile: serene. Like I don't care that this means I'm going to have to redo the report I just signed off on. Like being dragged back into this clusterfuck of a personal injury lawsuit potential isn't a drain on my time and resources.

"Before I forget, you need to restart your computer when you get back to your desk," Khent murmurs in an undertone to Janice.

The words are a little too softly toned for a work related conversation, but I let it slide because I'm leafing through the folder, a quick review before I start this meeting.

Janice's chair creaks as she leans a little closer to him, like I hadn't purposefully put their chairs six feet apart when I first set up the meeting room.

"What do you mean? It was working just fine when I left it," she whispers, not so quiet that I can't hear her.

"There's a system wide update that won't go through until everyone has restarted their computer. I checked what was holding it up, and you're the last to restart."

"Can it wait a little? I've got a lot of tabs open right now and I need all of them for what I'm currently working on," Janice returns, something oddly teasing in her voice for what she's saying.

I glance up from the file, taking in the way they're angled towards each other, like I'm not even here anymore.

"How long is a while?"

Janice tilts her head, surveying him with narrowed eyes and a hint of a smile. "Maybe a few days? My computer's running a little slow."

Khent gives a little breath of a laugh. "It's because you have too many tabs open."

"That's too bad, because I need all of them. Besides, I think I remember restarting my computer last week."

"You haven't restarted your computer in three weeks," Khent corrects her, voice dropping a little lower. "I did check your system uptime."

It takes me a few beats to realize that this isn't just normal couples bickering. Is it possible for discussing IT issues to be some kind of foreplay for these two?

I reign in my glare at Janice and Khent, who are very obviously not looking at me. They reek of their newly reformed mating bond, and I decide to torture them for this later. Preferably when I have a sinus infection and I don't have to smell the honeymoon phase on them.

I clear my throat, and the two of them jump, apparently having forgotten why they're here.

Janice's attention snaps to me, tearing away from the googly eyed stare she and Khent are making at each other. This is why I wrote the no-mate-bonding-with-coworkers policy a dozen years ago.

"Gwen!" she smiles back, looking a little uneasy. Possibly like she forgot I was here. Or because she can sense my immense displeasure.

I flip the manila folder's top shut, but it doesn't close, because there's too much fucking paperwork in here. I'm going to need to go to an office supplies store at some point to get more accordion folders, even if our office supply budget is overdrawn.

"Shall we get started?" I ask, but in the single second I let my hold on their attention lapse, they're already making goo-goo eyes at one another.

I don't want to do this anymore.

I never wanted to be in Monster Resources in the first place, but there aren't many jobs where my abilities can actually be put to use, and get PTO.

Still. Maybe it's time to put my notice in. I've worked here long enough.

After all, I could use something with better benefits.

1

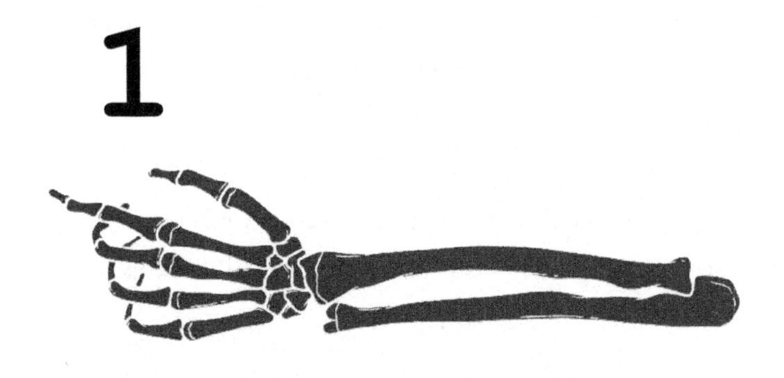

LOVE LAUGH LICH (Claws & Cubicles 1)

I never knew working at an office job would be this soul-sucking. I mean, everyone said it would be, and I expected some amount of sucking, but not like this.

It's one of those Tuesdays that feels a little too much like a second Monday. Specifically it feels like one of those Mondays that every little thing scratches against your consciousness like sandpaper on your face. The ticking of someone's watch. The creaky chairs that complain whenever someone shifts their weight a little. The smell of burnt coffee seeping out of the breakroom because putting the coffee pot directly beneath the drip is beyond some people.

I've never been an I-Hate-Mondays kind of person, but I think I might be turning into one, this very Tuesday.

It could just be because the washed out fluorescent lighting is giving me a headache. The conversation two cubicles over, the not-so-subtle whispering about vacation days, is making my eyes roll back in my skull. I can't focus on my spreadsheets. I'm not used to working with so many other people around. Maybe the reason I never contemplated hating my coworkers is because I wasn't with them for the whole day before. The only thing I'm capable of thinking about is how much I want to poke my head up over the divider and ask for some quiet.

Suddenly, I get my wish.

All the chatter silences, a sudden hush that feels heavy and old as a catacomb. A feeling like a breeze ripples through the room, as my skin prickles. An unnatural cold wraps around my body, when I see a dark shadow fall over me.

I look up into the hollow cowl of a black cloak that drapes down to the floor.

The spectre hangs near me with an empty stare that feels like standing on the edge of a cliff.

"Any messages, Lily?" the disembodied voice murmurs, low and guttural, coming from somewhere within the black robes that billow even without wind.

"I, uh, no, but I have a couple things people asked to reschedule," I stammer, shuffling through my desk for the little paper squares I've jotted down notes. I pause before I relay them to him, glancing around. I can see the color-drained faces of my coworkers peering out over their partitions to watch.

We usually do this in my office, but it's currently being renovated. I mean, I don't really have an office. I have a desk in the little waiting room outside the Dark Lich Lord's Grand Sanctum, where I sit and reschedule his appointments, remind him to take his daily blood doses, and really just tell people it'll be another ten minutes before they can see him.

At least, I used to have a desk. Until an assassin managed to sneak past security and tried to ambush the Lich Lord in the waiting room. It got messy. As in, pretty much all of the furniture was obliterated in the fight messy. I'd stepped away from my desk, only to return to a scorched room and a pile of cinders. Honestly, I don't even know why we have security if the Lich Lord can just vaporize anyone that comes at him with a poisoned blade.

There was a "chosen hero" or whatever a few years ago that tried to defeat the Lich Lord, but it didn't quite work out. There were details, but that kind of stuff gets buried in the endless paperwork that is required in maintaining an evil dominion. I don't think anyone has the real story except the Lich Lord himself.

Anyway, that's how I got stuck in one of the spare partitioned desks in the accounting department. It's only until the room is finished being renovated.

I glance over my shoulder and at the whole office still staring, unsubtly, to see what's going on.

It's right about then that I realize, most people in the Dark Domain don't get to see their Lich Lord all that often.

"Um, I'll bring these to the Sanctum, shall I?" I say, feeling their stares on my back.

Still, their stares are nothing compared to the gravity I feel when I look into the empty depth that is the Lich's cloak. The constant motion of his cloak is a slow, underwater-like movement that always makes me start to lean towards him. It's a weird, dizzying feeling. People talk about staring into the void until the void stares back, but that void is always staring.

The cloak's cowl nods stiffly, but the cold air of his presence feels more like an appreciative caress.

My chair makes an awful screech as I push it back against the floor; the sounds of me packing up my things from the desk are the only noises in the office. I dodge around a few desks and hurry after the Lich Lord to the Grand Sanctum.

Some people really haven't adjusted to life under the Dark Reign of Terror yet. Some things are different, but honestly it's all cosmetic. Things aren't that different from when we had a normal, living CEO.

And the thing about economic collapse and social upheaval is that there's a lot of room for upward mobility. At least that's what Janice from HR says, and I guess she's right, because I used to work in customer service, but now I'm a personal assistant to the Lich.

The Grand Sanctum is an utterly gorgeous room, once you get used to how creepy it is. It's about as big as a ballroom, but much more cluttered. The walls are lined with old bookshelves stuffed with dusty tomes and piled scrolls, occasionally featuring distilling glasses, crystals and jars of murky liquids. The windows are all stained glass in geometric patterns, all blue and green and purple. They don't let much light in, but they're my favorite part about stepping into the Dark Lord's office.

As the twenty-foot carved door shuts closed behind me, I start reading off the notes for today's schedule, the missives for him that I've sorted through by priority.

I get through maybe two of them before I realize the Dark Lord isn't listening in the slightest. Usually he interjects, making me take down notes about rearranging things or moving appointments up. I've never gotten this far without him at least canceling something.

He's pacing the lower inner level of the Sanctum, the ritual floor. It's drawn up in runes and incantation circles, with all his most-used ingredients lined up near the edges, and an altar for sacrifices in the center.

"...And there's that initiative to bring more women into STEM fields. That's Sneakiness, Traumatization, Evil Studies, and Misfortune," I trail off, watching his movement.

Definitely not listening.

"Is something the matter, Soven?" I ask. I don't usually use his first name, only when we're in his office together. I think it amuses him that he, an ageless entity with power beyond comprehension, is on a first name basis with a mortal like me. It's that social upheaval at work.

At that, the Dark Lord pauses in his pacing. He doesn't turn to look at me.

"Was it the assassination attempt?"

He gives a nod, and his cloak flutters like a sigh disturbs them. "Yes. I'm afraid it's left me somewhat unbalanced."

"It did cause quite a disruption. I've already briefed the legal department; they're working on how to deal with the agency that sent her. They've got some plans for a lawsuit, and some other options for how we should vet our outsourced labor in the future," I say.

That covers all the important concerns, but I wonder a bit if he hates having to seek me out at my new desk as much as I hate having to work there. After a moment I add, “I’m told the renovation should be finished in a few days.”

He tilts his hood towards me in a way that feels reminiscent of a wry smile. “Sometimes I wonder who really is the Evil Overlord around here.”

I contain a smile at the burst of pride. “I don't know what you mean,” I say, shrugging, putting on a tone of utmost innocence.

“Well I didn't hire you for your looks,” he starts to say, and cuts himself off. The cloak stiffens in something like a wince. “Not that I wouldn't. Or that there's anything wrong with your looks. They're very nice for a human. It's just not reign-policy to hire specifically on an appearance-basis-”

I smother a giggle behind my hand. “Quit while you're ahead.”

Sometimes I really think the whole dark and ominous presence he exudes is just a front behind which he hides his social ineptitude. No one would exactly cower in terror at him if they knew he was kind of a dork.

The feeling of my smile fades as I watch him. If I thought there were shoulders under that cloak of perpetual billowing, I would have thought they’d sunk down in frustration.

“I’m at a loss, Lily,” he says, the cloak’s hood turning to look deep into one of the greenish fires. “For how to complete this ritual.”

My eyes fall to the ritual circle. Now that he brings it up, it does look about the same as I saw it arranged last week. Usually things get moved around, new symbols drawn on it, etc.

"If you need me to order more ingredients, I can take down a list," I begin, wondering where I'm going to get a copy of the requisition forms when my usual desk is now ash.

But Soven shakes his head.

"There are many magical things that can't be collected in vials," Soven explains. "A last breath. A first kiss. A shiver over the skin."

I fall silent, his words provoking my imagination. I don't know much about magic, and he's never told me much about how he does what he does.

"Last week, the woman who was in the waiting room, before I—" he jerks his head and makes a clicking noise with his teeth, referring back to the vaporization event, "But these assassins are becoming craftier by the day, they must have infiltrated that agency. There's no knowing who I can trust, now."

I nod. Initially, we had hired the woman through an agency, had her vetted for her services through them. I hadn't really known what services exactly she was supposed to provide at the time, and when my brain puts two together, I nearly laugh.

“Hang on, is that what you needed? A shiver?” I ask skeptically. “That’s what we’re outsourcing for?”

The cloak’s hood turns slowly to me, and he nods.

I’m doing my best to keep my face straight. I let out a quiet laugh as I say, “You could have just called me in. I’ve got skin.”

I wonder if that last remark is rude or something. After all, he doesn’t really have skin, to my knowledge. I hope I don’t have to take an undead sensitivity training class now.

The cloak’s hood stares through me for a few long, uncomfortable moments. The air doesn’t grow colder, instead I’m too warm about the collar, and maybe it’s not anything supernatural, my face is reddening under the intensity of his attention.

Every second in the hourglass slipping by makes me think my suggestion was perhaps really dumb. I don’t know, maybe he needed a professional to shiver for him. Maybe professionally rendered shivers are higher quality? I’ve never really thought about it before.

“You do,” he notes, something different in his voice. He’s looking at me, and I don’t think he’s ever stared at me this long.

Is he looking at my skin? Everything that isn’t covered by my office clothes, my arms and shins and my collar, all of it feels oddly on display. I fight the urge to cross my arms over myself or any other way of covering myself up.

"You do," he repeats, crossing the Sanctum towards me, less like he's moving towards me, more like the room is shrinking the space between us. With him comes that scent of herbs, a heavy dose of clove, thyme, lavender, cedar, and a slight hint of embalming fluids.

"Yeah, I do," I echo, my voice nearly a whisper and more than enough for how close we are. Either I feel like I'm underwater with him or I feel that I'm in over my head. Maybe I'm not as used to being in my boss's presence as I think I am, because by now I'd usually have gone back to my little not-a-real-office.

He towers over me, staring into my soul probably. I mean, as far as I can tell, the cloak's hood doesn't have eyeballs, but even as I look into that endless void, I can feel his gaze sweeping over me, sending goosebumps over my skin.

His head tilts ever so slightly, like he can tell.

When my coworkers talk about the chills Soven gives them, it's all 'frailty of life' this, and 'acute sense of my mortality' that.

And for an undying Lord of Darkness, that makes sense.

But when he looks at me, I get this feeling like walking through an old house, where all the furniture has sheets draped over them while the house is dormant, and suddenly, someone is dragging the sheets off. Like he's unveiling me; like plucking petals off a flower, to see what's hiding at the center.

"You would really do that," he says, unconvinced. He makes it sound like I'm chopping off an arm.

"Shiver-rly isn't dead yet," I say, trying a wide smile. It feels like the best thought I've had today, until I hear myself say it and wince. I cough. "Uh. Yeah. It's no big deal."

He's still for a long moment, before he nods. He tilts his head to the ritual floor. "Come then."

It's then, creeping down into the ritual floor, careful not to step on any of the lines, that I realize I've never been so far into this room. Maybe I'm too used to being able to duck back out the door as soon as I'm done.

Standing by the Sanctum doors, hugging the walls, is an entirely different experience from crossing to the middle, which borders on agoraphobic. I've never needed the closeness of my flimsy cubicle walls so much. The sound of my breath echoes off the tiles, the only sound in the hall, making me feel like I should maybe hold my breath. My footsteps against the marble punctuate the air so loud I nearly wince with each one.

I hike my skirt up a bit as I hop onto the altar Soven gestures to, straightening it as I sit down and lay back.

The stone is cold to touch, and there's something about laying across this ledge in the center of the room that makes me feel more than exposed. How can I feel practically naked with all my clothes still on?

Maybe it's the giant mirror on the ceiling.

It's pretty high up, but I can see myself, wavy brown hair spread around me, the lush dark green of my skirt. It's too far away to see my freckles or birthmarks, or the buttons on my blouse.

Oh shit, I think my nipples are hard because it's so damn cold in the ritual space. I try to inconspicuously crane my head up for a better look to check if they're visible through my blouse.

"Everything all right?" Soven asks, crossing to my side.

"Yes!" I squeak, a little too quickly. Ugh.

His voice is deeper than the abyss. When he talks to me, sometimes his words reverberate down my body and find all my hollow spaces. Too often I find it's left me biting my lip.

It's hard for me to believe there's absolutely nothing under that cloak. There's gotta be at least bones or something. I speculated as much to Janice from HR once, and she laughed, "Why, so you can jump those bones?"

Suffice it to say, I haven't told anyone about what his voice does to me or my thoughts about what he really looks like. I pretend not to think about my undead boss in any unprofessional way.

"Just lay back and relax," he intones, like he's used to doing this. He must be, he's done probably hundreds of rituals, and this is my first. "Close your eyes."

There is something soothing in the way he flips through pages of his tomes, muttering incantations as he sprinkles herbs and splashes of potions into the cold burning fire.

As soothing as listening to him move about is, I can't help but feel the moments stretch thin with curiosity and anticipation. I wonder how he's going to make me shiver. I'd think the easiest way would be to turn the thermostat way down, but he seems to have a more arcane approach.

I almost startle out of my skin when his touch ghosts down my bare shoulder. A whisper crawls up my neck, and I feel something soft, something almost like skin with a light down of fur over it. It's like the soft side of cured leather, but alive.

I shiver alright. I shiver right down to my godsdamnned vagina, that moth-wing flutter low in my belly as my clit pulses awake with interest. The need for him to drag that touch, mouth or whatever it is, over more of my body is so visceral, I nearly moan.

If he couldn't tell my nipples were hard through my bra before, I'm almost absolutely sure he can now.

I can feel the magic buzzing in the air as the last ingredient completes the ritual, but I keep my eyes squeezed shut. I've seen the light blaze from under the door when he's done rituals before.

The air abates, and after a few minutes I hope it's safe enough to peek around. When I look up again, his attention is buried back in his books, as he scribbles something down.

I guess he doesn't need me now, and I should probably get back to work.

Still, I pause when I get to the door, glancing back at him.

"…I've never been kissed, either," I say after a moment.

It's true. A few years ago, a fortune teller told me that my soulmate was the champion who would overthrow the Dark Reign. And I, a naïve dummy at the time, believed her. I should have seen then that it was a load of crock to get me to waste more money on her tarot booth, but it kept me saving that kiss for the chosen one. By the time there were rumors of his death, I'd realized what a fool I'd been. It was hard to get close to anybody at that, when the takeover and acquisition happened, there was so much chaos. After that, well, I was too busy being Soven's personal assistant.

I feel foolish saying it, not because I'm ashamed of being a virgin or whatever, but because who says that to her boss?

I duck out the door before he can say anything, before he can see the way my cheeks turn red, and hopefully before he realizes how much I want him to be that first kiss.

More Things By Kate Prior

Love Laugh Lich (Claws & Cubicles 1)

Lily has been the Lich's secretary ever since his evilness took over the company. She loves her job, but she's got some questions about her boss. Like what's under that cloak of ever-billowing.

Her wondering intensifies when one day the Lich needs something from her that isn't just scheduling appointments--but a shiver. He needs it for a spell, but it feels like it crosses a line from their usual banter.

After her contributions to his dark rituals become more than OSHA compliant, sex-magic-and-triple-cocks-oh-my, she starts to contemplate whether the Lich Lord returns her feelings, or still only sees her as his secretary.

Lily may have given him her body, but he never asked for her heart.

Meet Me at the Anvil

When Diane faints during her wedding vows, it's expected. Her family thinks almost everything is too stimulating for her because of her fainting condition. Of course they matched her with a man who couldn't make anyone's heart flutter.

When her fiancé tries to make light of the situation by giving her a fainting goat, the ridicule is too much to bear.

Diane wants more than the life before her— she wants to live the passion and adventure she's only ever found in the erotic sketches she creates, and the kind of heart-racing feelings her fiancé's cousin and best man Liam gives her.

The last thing Diane expects as she flees from the church, however, is for the best man to run away with her.

If you enjoy learning about the craft of writing or finding solidarity in the ups and downs of publishing, listen to the podcast *Romance Writer's Therapy*, hosted by Kate Prior and Marty Vee.

You can follow Kate on socials, Instagram, Twitter, or Tiktok @bykateprior, or join her reader's group on Facebook, *Kate's Priory of Paranormal Romance.*

Find book updates, content warnings, or subscribe to her newsletter at kate-prior.com.

Made in United States
North Haven, CT
20 April 2023